"Stylish and provocative … a tantalizing reflection on living the contradictions in every identity and of definitively knowing what is real."

Giller Prize, Jury Citation

"Simply brilliant … A dazzling brain-puzzle of a story."

Maclean's Magazine

"Brilliant … while Schofield has digested all of postmodernism's tics and tricks, her writing is fundamentally empathetic … as an avant-garde novelist, Schofield is in a class unto herself." *Globe & Mail*

"Exhilarating … startlingly vivid and positively adrenal."

National Post

"Schofield's trademark Celtic-Gothic sensibility is evident once again as *Martin John* explores madness, dark comedy, isolation and sexual compulsion." *Toronto Star*

"Fearless … Schofield pushes the boundaries in careful calibrations of narrative structure and language that bites." *Vancouver Sun*

"Schofield's first achievement is to burrow into Martin John's rackety mind. Her second crucial achievement is to turn this unsettling apprehension into a necessary, extraordinary act of empathy."

The Winnipeg Review

"Hold your breath while reading this novel. The story transgresses the body with or without our permission, and illuminates important ideas we ordinarily look away from. And yet it is now, more than ever, that we need to reread the body."

Lidia Yuknavitch, author of *The Chronology of Water*

"*Martin John* is singular in contemporary literature … moving, profoundly human, insightful, and darkly humorous."

Thalia Field, author of *Bird Lovers, Backyard*

PRAISE FOR *MALARKY*

"A caustic, funny, and moving fantasia of an Irish mammy going round the bend." **Emma Donoghue, author of *Room***

"Mid-guffaw you may find that you've taken it all most intensely to heart. I read *Malarky* over a year ago and Our Woman is still with me." **Helen Oyeyemi, author of *Boy, Snow, Bird***

"A fine first novel." **Margaret Atwood, author of *The Heart Goes Last***

"*Malarky* is a terrific read, a brilliant collision of heartbreak and hilarity written in a voice that somehow seems both feral and perfectly controlled. Anakana Schofield's Our Woman takes a cool nod at Joyce, then goes her own way in one of the most moving and lyrical debut novels I've read." **Jess Walter, author of *Beautiful Ruins***

"This is the story of Anakana Schofield's teapot-wielding 'Our Woman': fretful mother, disgruntled farmwife, and—surprisingly late in life—sexual outlaw/anthropologist. Everything about this primly raunchy, uproarious novel is unexpected—each draught poured from the teapot marks another moment of pure literary audacity." **Lynn Coady, author of *The Antagonist***

"One of the delights of this novel is the language in which it is written … it is boldly not fifty shades of anything. I admire Schofield's ability to pull off something so difficult with charm and brio." ***The Guardian***

"Schofield's portrait of a woman whose personality is beginning to fragment after a lifetime in an emotional vacuum is both blackly comic and deeply felt. There is something heroic about the desperate resilience of Our Woman, and the originality of her depiction by Schofield, that leaves an indelible trace on the reader's mind." ***Sunday Telegraph***

"The most distinctive novel of its kind I've read in a decade." ***Irish Central***

MARTIN JOHN

Anakana Schofield

LOS ANGELES · HIGH WYCOMBE

First published as *Martin John* in 2015 by Biblioasis, Canada

This edition published by And Other Stories, 2016
High Wycombe, England
www.andotherstories.org

ISBN 9781908276667
eBook ISBN 9781908276674

A catalogue record for this book is available from the British Library.

Editor: John Metcalf; Copy-editor: Emily Donaldson; Typesetter: Kate Hargreaves; Typefaces: Adobe Garamond and Verlag; Cover Design: Hannah Naughton; Cover Image: Pamela Joe McFarlane; Printed and bound by the CPI Group (UK) Ltd, Croydon, CRO 4YY.

Supported using public funding by
ARTS COUNCIL
ENGLAND

For Jenny Diski and Marie-Lulu Corbeau
"Work works"

"For the rest of the week, all was calm. What might possibly have troubled the peace? . . . And what cause did he have to be particularly grumpy? . . . Strolling to the post office was always quite enjoyable."

—Robert Walser, *The Assistant*

"Rage—Goddess, sing the rage of Peleus' son Achilles,
murderous, doomed, that cost the Achaeans countless losses,
hurling down to the House of Death so many sturdy souls,
great fighters' souls, but made their bodies carrion,
feasts for the dogs and birds,
and the will of Zeus was moving toward its end."

—Homer, *The Iliad*, 1.1–6

Index

1. Martin John has made mistakes.
2. Check my card.
3. Rain will fall.
4. Harm was done.
5. *It* put me in the Chair.

WHAT THEY DON'T KNOW:

Flashing is a very angry act.

Rain will fall.
Check my card.
I never tasted bread like the bread in Beirut.
I don't read the fucken Daily Telegraph.

WHAT THEY KNOW:

Martin John has not been to Beirut.
He has only been to London and to visit his Aunty Noanie.

The dentist's waiting room shaped Martin John's life. A simple room, nothing to suggest it contained the almighty power it did.

It could have been any 5 or 15 minutes in any youth's lifetime.

He remembered the strange fluorescent light, the organized nature of the room and how odd (it was) for a country dental practice to be so well planned inside a house: treatment room + waiting room. The physical space, so carefully executed, had made him comfortable and sleepy.

Surely to God they'd come. They'd come for him.
She continued to give him the line.
In the hope he might take it.
That he had gone to help that girl.

⋯→

There were rumours.
Other rumours.
Other girls.
Other moments.
Same boy.

Martin John is living in England now.

In London.

South London.

Off Tower Bridge Road in an enclave of tiny houses, on a slit of a street, at number 7 Cluny Place.

Once, early on, in London, Martin John was vague about the time he went to sleep. Mam told him straight: Get a job at night.

Get a job at night or else I'll come for ya.

I don't know, he said.
To every question he said he did not know.
Still they came, the questions came.
I don't know did not put a stop to them.
He has to know, she said.
He had to know because he was in the room.
If you are in the room Martin John then you know.
Unless you weren't in the room?
Were you not in the room, she suggests.
Had you gone to the toilet?
Were you (maybe) in the toilet?
I was in the room, he said.
I was in the room and I still don't know, he said.

⋯→

Remember for me, she said another time not long after it. Remember would you? It will help us if you remember. We can help you if you remember. The guard had told her to use the word *we*. If you could get to him with *we* then we can all help him, he had said. He was a nice enough guard. Had a bit of a red rash on his neck, high blood pressure, but pushing through. That kind of man. The kind of man who pushed through. She imagined pushing through, pushing on, pushing these problems away. Did he have a son? He did. What would he do in her situation? I'll tell you what I'd do, the guard said. I'd keep at him. He has to remember and we'll wait until he does.

Those were the early days. The early-on days when there was patience for him, when there was patience for a man who was really only a boy then. Not anymore. All patience expired.

Tell me again what you remember of the chair and the girl? Tell it to me slowly. Remember how you moved over to help her, to let her know her skirt was hitched. Did you pull it down? You did. Did you maybe pull it down now? To afford her decency? You were trying to help her, weren't you?
I don't know mama, I don't know.
Why are you calling me that? She snaps.

⋯→

Still he maintained he didn't know.
Was he lying?
Or does he simply not know?
When is she going to tell us what he knows?
How long will we wait only to find out like the last time that she doesn't know either what he doesn't know?
Are you feeling cheated? Frustrated?
Imagine the people that had to interview him.
Oh they eventually interview them. Eventually they trip up and there's no avoiding an arrest or an interview.
He went a long time without an interview though.
Much longer than he should have.

⋯→

Watch her. She's telling us things.
She has started. Begun early. Is it going to be like the last time?
Will he do it again?
Will she do it to us again? We're hopeful.
Is she going to disappoint us?

⋯→

Mam was wrong about Cluny Place. She read the map poorly. It's only a bicycle ride from Waterloo Station. Very central. He doesn't have to sit in tunnels. He can take the bus, strange routes past the cricket ground at Kennington. He can head South to Brixton where he eats spicy patties when his mind is at him. If his mouth is hot, his mind is distracted. He likes his mouth burning hot.

There's two cafes on Tower Bridge Road. At one, he can get a fry. At the other a pork pie.
This is what Martin John eats.

The newsagent across the road is for his papers. That's all he needs. Pork and papers are what he needs.

He has the bike.
She doesn't want him on public transport.
Don't go near the buses, they might see you on the buses and don't go down on the Tube for you could go into a tunnel and never come out.
D'ya hear me Martin John?

Did he have a role in it?
Did she have a role in it?
Do you have a role in it?
Should they?
Do you think?

⇢

Mam repeatedly asks whether or not he can hear her—*d'ya hear me Martin John?* Because we can assume she doesn't feel heard. She doesn't want to hear what it is he would say, if he were to speak the truth. She saw a man on telly once. She has seen plenty men on telly, but this one frightened her. She has seen many men on telly who frighten her. But he frightened her in a particular way. He frightened her the way she feels frightened when she sees someone lash out at a dog. In actual fact, she's not a woman easily frighted. The dark, insects, vermin, death, moths in the flour—none bother her.

But a glance, a moment, in which there's an indication of what might be the truth of a person sits longer at her. A rat would run under the cupboard sooner than look at you. A man or woman who lets a boot fly at a dog or throws an item at a chicken in their way has a raw and sealed-in-something that she's convinced can never be dislodged. That man on the television made her afraid because she recognized something of her son in him. There were many who talked of their crimes in that programme. They talked like they were uncomfortable ingredients in a recipe. Something hard to shop for like chopped walnuts, ground lemon rind or tamarind. They used the names of the crime, I murdered, I raped, I killed, I punched. Not him. The details are gone. He talked above and around his crime. He remained oblivious or chose oblivion. He was unsure why he was in here. He did not say he hadn't done it. He did not say it was a mistake. He merely said nothing either way. They showed this man beside a man with a long ponytail, who said he had opted for chemical castration and then physical castration. He was the only one in that prison program who had availed of it. She thought of a small boy, being born, riding a trike, building a fort and then flash-forward all these years. She wondered if that boy building an' deploying could ever image-forward to the man they might grow up to be. Was it that she thought criminals should suffer unto perpetuity? She thought maybe it was.

Then she pushed it all aside. It was distressing that a stranger, in another time zone, filtered through a televisual tube, could induce this in her. She returned to *it* being a mistake, a misunderstanding, messing gone wrong, (boys get up to stuff), which it was. Martin John was young and *it* was only messing.

If people coming down a televisual tube were going to disturb her it would be a long disturbance.

What about it?

She did not like the idea she had a role in it.
You would not like the idea you had a role in it.
Did she have a role in it?
Have you had a role in it?
Do you have a role in this?

These are some of the questions a mother may ask herself.

Another interview, Tuesday morning radio this time, had her by the ear. An interview with a former drug-addicted mother, who wondered if the fact *she was an addict* was the reason her son grew up to become a drug dealer and robbed a post office in Kiltimagh. It was a strange place to rob a post office, said a priest who happened to be in there trying to buy a stamp. They wondered if her son did it because he'd been watching too much American television. The mother admitted the son glamourized his violence and boosted his profile with the words that the "feds" were after him. The mother admitted she thought the "feds" was a parcel company. I thought he thought he was being *chased* by the post office. I see different now. How did he get there, the priest on the panel asked. He took the bus, the radio-mother said. The woman interviewing them all said words like Now I realize this is very difficult for you all.

Except it wasn't difficult for the priest. He was not at fault. Nor was it difficult for the Minister of Justice who was on the line. The only person it was difficult for was that mother with the veins from which her son had grown and robbed a post office. There was an advert where the radio-mother spoke to tempt the audience to keep listening, *I botched up motherhood* her voice said. Find out after the break, Did she botch up motherhood? annunciated the presenter. Martin John's mam turned the radio off.

As Martin John's mam hears the former drug-addicted mother puzzle it out, she recognizes there are many mothers out there puzzling things out. She will have to be a mother who puzzles. Except she is not the type who puzzles. She prefers to head, bang, to a conclusion. In this case: I was not that mother. I am not that mother. I didn't raise my son to rob a post office. So what did she raise him to?

She prays hard. She incants for him. Once she prayed to St Jude, a man who fell in his own way, so he'd understand this overwhelming need to keep her son straight. I can't afford no three-time-cock-crowing with Martin John, one more crowing and it's prison he'll be.

Everything I do and have done is to keep him on the outside. Sure if it's in he goes, they'll kill him. Plain and simple. They'd eat him alive, they don't spare the like of him. Someday he'll come home to me. He'll come home when he's failing or an old fella and I'll be waiting.

···➔

She's probably lying.

She doesn't want him near her.

Ever again.

Some days she dreams/imagines/fantasizes he might be killed. Shot or run over by a bus.

Like them fellas you read about in the papers.

Sometimes they kill men like him. Others do it. They hunt and they kill them. Sometimes they wait 'til they're inside. Sometimes they leave a note on them.

Martin John's not as bad as the ones they kill.

She reminds, comforts herself.

Martin John's mam hasn't factored her own aging into it. She'll never age, only waits on him to come home to her.

Three times a year she summons him. Always by ferry: Sealink not B&I. She doesn't trust anything with a B in it. B&B never, B&Q—won't go near it. She even wavers over BBC. B gave me trouble my whole life is all she'll say. That's what she'll say on B.

We can suspect Martin John's father's name began with the letter B. Was he Brendan or Brian or just a simple Bob? A simple disappearing Bob.

⋯➤

There will be five refrains. The Index tells us there will be five refrains. We can conclude these five refrains may or may not take us into the circuits.

1. Martin John has made mistakes.
2. Check my card.
3. Rain will fall.
4. Harm was done.
5. *It* put me in the Chair.

There may be subsidiary refrains: I don't read the fucken *Daily Telegraph*. We will do as the Index tells us this time. There could be involuntary refrains, about which, alas, not much can be done, unless you take a pencil to them. When will she tell us exactly what they mean? She may not, since the mother may not ever know why he did what he did, or why it was her son and not the woman up the road's son. There are simply going to be things we won't know. It's how it is. As it is in life must it be unto the page. There's the known and the unknown. In the middle is where we wander and wonder.

⋯➔

Sometimes he said he hadn't a clue, but he'd think about it. It was the difference between Martin John and the others. He offers to think about it when she asks him. A man who was pure evil wouldn't make any such offer, would he?

He did hear her. Yes, he understood. He understood whatever it was he did, he would not do *it* again.

What was it? She wanted to know. What was it? Tell me what *it* was.

I have no clue, he said honestly, I've no clue at all. But he promised he would think about it.

⋯→

Was that refrain number 1 or 2?

There's no refrain called *I have no clue*. This is an interruption. Martin John does not like interruptions.

THE PAPERS

The newspaper will always matter to Martin John.

He won't be a day without it and it won't be a day without him.

It mattered before the "difficult time" and it matters today. The stability of it, the regularity, the newspaper women sustain him.

It's why he calls into Euston on his way to work. Or, first thing every morning, if he's not working, he'll cross to the newsagents on Tower Bridge Road. The *Irish Times* he gathers each day at Euston, except Sunday, and a second British broadsheet, the choice of which he rotates, based on the headlines or the pictures of the columnists. There are a few frumpies he has no time for. There are photos and headlines and certain words that worry Martin John and he will not buy what worries him, because his mother has warned him not to.

Martin John how many times have I told you, give up the papers when they're worrying you, you cannot be in them if they're worrying.

He never buys a newspaper if he notices a headline has petrol in it. Or pervert. He's not keen on P words.

⋯➤

The first page he reads is the letters page to see did any of his letters get through?

In John Menzies at Euston, amid the wefty drift of chips and cooking croissants from next door, he takes thoughtful time to select exactly the newspaper he wants, unhurried by the arms reaching around to grab the pink and flush *Financial Times*, or those who fold the newspaper abruptly. Stare.

The second thing he checks: the crossword clues. If they're terrible—determined by reading 3 across and only 2 of the down (they're always weaker on the down), then he chooses a different paper. The newspaper determines many things in Martin John's daily life.

You'll only depress yourself his mother has warned him. *This country is gone to the dogs. It's beyond the dogs, there's not even the brick of a dog track left. Sure they've lifted the dirt from under our feet.*

She never says specifically what's wrong with the country, only offers the hint of cut-price airfares and suited-up Bucket-Air-gobshites and the price and rush of everyone. She blames it all on a man called Tony.

At least the dogs have a number on them. It's more than can be said for the humans creeping their way about and giving no hint to whatever they're hatching. They'd never give you that bit of information about themselves them fellas. You'd have to take their number.

⋯→

She may be right about the dogs, but she's lost the way
with Martin John. She birthed him, raised him to obedi-
ence but never forgave the times he disobeyed.

*Keep your hands to yourself and you'll know well where
they are.*

He did not keep his hands to himself.

⋯→

He phones her every Sunday, in the phone box, outside
Waterloo Station. Most of the weekly events in Martin
John's life take place outside or inside train stations. It's
always raining when he phones and she can hear it. His
money's religiously running out, but she never offers to
phone him back. *Not at all, it'd only upset him, be an insult
to the man.* Martin John is a proud son. Hold on, he'll say,
'til I put another fifty pence in. She raised her son proud
and she won't upset him. She will not.

She's always been wrong about Martin John, it's why the
phone calls surprised her. Today she's wrong about Martin
John: he's not buying the paper to study the news. It
couldn't possibly depress him any further, it has much more
serious input than that. He's dependent on it. *Directed by it.*
He cannot calculate the depressive and improbable nature
of mankind without it. For if he were to stop reading and
thinking and wondering, then there'd be little reason to
walk the streets at all. The newspaper is the only thing that
cements his arrival at work each day or the raising of his
head off the pillow.

That need to go and buy it keeps him buoyed. Keeps him
from the *situations.* Mam said only a structured daily life
would achieve this. He's keen to avoid the situations, a lot of
trouble they caused and "shaming" for his mam. She doesn't

like it when he calls her from the hospital phone. Not at all.

Keep yourself on the outside, Martin John.

What are you doing in that place? What has you in there at all? Tell me what is happening, Martin John? And the only rabble that would come back from him down the line was that old religious rabble. A rabble she didn't raise him to, she'd insist.

I didn't raise you to be saying this. Put that phone down right now. Phone me back when you've sense to make. But as soon as he'd go to replace the receiver she'd shriek at him in a vocal register akin to a buzzard's.

If you dare put down this phone on me Martin John as God is my judge I won't be forgiven for what I'll do. Come here to me and heed my words and if you don't I'll tell those fellas to lock you up. D'ya hear now?

He heard, he never failed to hear, the bellow of incarceration and he was certain the paper, the walks, the guarding, every miserable minute of it was preferable to incarceration.

Martin John has a personal relationship with several journalists writing in the paper. The capital letter of the first- and surnames he imprints to a shortened form, so Caitlin Boylan would be CB, or Barry Hutchinson is BH and Phil O'Toole is POT. During one situation he thought he and BH were having tea together, so he's a bit wary of him since, doesn't read his words too closely, lest they set him off again. He subsequently discovered BH had nothing to say. BH has gone away off to some hot place in Afghanistan the last few weeks, so it's easy avoid him on the page. He was in China too for a while. There's another strident Madam in the paper, Anna-something, who bothers him. She's lovely hair, rides a bicycle, but complains non-stop and is ferocious over the fellas. Wants them expelled out of Ireland, the way that other writer (whose name he never says aloud) desires a cull on women. The two of them should be married and diminish the population, he thinks.

This is the kind of chuckle and sustenance the papers give him—and words, he receives his daily words, sometimes they take him to the dictionary. He tallies up the number of words that commence with a chosen letter each day and records them in a line. At work he has a big dictionary hidden in the drawer. The other guard has a stack of filthy magazines that live under Martin John's dictionary. He's to use a handkerchief to lift his dictionary up and carefully replace the top magazine upside down, so the photos don't set him off.

Careful, careful, careful.

Carefully does it, Martin John, the way mam has trained him.

Caitlin might call him MJ if they were ever on speaking terms. He doesn't think much of her harping on about her boyfriend trouble and her wine glasses and her dining-room table. But he has a file on her.

He's a file on all of them.

The majority of his files though are on the Eurovision Song Contest.

He has traced the ancestry of their names and he can see certainly a pattern in the (kinds of) people who put words on the newspaper page. He'd like to put a stop to it, but he accepts he can't control everything.

Martin John accepts. Martin John accepts.
He accepted a lot in those days.
He accepts a lot these days.
(But does he accept the truth?)

⸺➤

A strange week. One strange week, among the many strange weeks, was all it took for Martin John to change the rules on P words. It was incredible he could isolate it as a single strange week given the extended years of strange weeks. Did he have an ear infection perhaps? Instead of avoiding them P and p words, he isolates them. Isolates them into long lists. For you. Now. So you know he's kept busy, so you don't have to worry he might be beside you on the Tube, or following you about, or thinking about your body parts. He's thinking only about words with P at the start. So you do not need to worry about what else he has been thinking about. He has only thought about P words.

Here's the evidence.

POSSIBLE, PAISLEY, POLITICAL, POLITICIAN, POLITI-CAL, POLITICIANS, PEOPLE, PART, PAY, PARLIAMENT, POINTED, PILLS, PATENT, POTENT, PAIN, PLUMMET.

Martin John focuses on those who employ the letter P excessively. He keeps score, tallies them up. It keeps him very, very busy. He needs to be busy. If he's busy he won't slip up. If he's busy, they won't come for him.

Also, he is directed by the news, remember. If you are worried about what he might be up to keep your eye on the headlines. Potters Bar was where it all went sour. Note he did not ever see the P-word in Potters Bar.

⋯➔

You're involved now. You have a role. See? You are watching the headlines for him. You are forecasting like the Index forecasts.

⋯➔

Wednesday, every week, Martin John catches the train —the 2:30 pm—to Hatfield to visit his Aunty Noanie. Noanie is blessed to live in a council flat that stares out onto another block. She has fabric and doilies under everything and this suggests to him she's done well for herself. The place hums with old cooking smells that follow him home and remain inside his nose for days. Noanie has a man, but he's never about and Martin John never asks after him because mam warned him not to.

He's always on the 5:30 pm train back and they share an exchange as he's leaving, that *he'd better go, you wouldn't know what way the trains might be*, but he knows exactly the way the trains do be. He knows them down to their slide and squeal and hiss and beep, beep, beep, and huss again and that slide, the diligent tug back to London.

And for Martin John, the tug doesn't come a minute too soon. For if he were trapped at Noanie's by bad weather that wouldn't do at all. If it snowed, that would scupper him, or if there were leaves on the line that could interrupt things. The thought of staying the night with Noanie frightens him more than catching TB. There's no inoculation against Noanie and the thought of her dislodging the distributed fabric to put down a bed for him.

So each Wednesday he checks the weather before he departs very, very carefully and examines the sky, to help him predict whether rain may fall or if he might need to cancel the visit.

If it seems that Martin John leads a regimented kind of existence, it's because he does lead a regimented existence, where he leaves nothing open to the palm of possibility. He does not suit possibility. He learnt that during the difficult time. He's better now, smarter too. He's careful now.

WHAT THEY KNOW:

Martin John has refrains

WHAT THEY DON'T KNOW:

Refrains can give way to circuits

He doesn't like Meddlers. A Meddler got Martin John into trouble. More than once. If you are a Meddler, he won't like you. That's the way it is. How will you know if you are a Meddler?

Check my Card.

The Boss likes Martin John. He likes him for one reason. Martin John is reliable. He is never late and rarely off sick. Martin John knows this. His onion is on the pan.

If Dallas hadn't stacked the papers that one way, that one time, things might well have turned out differently on the job.

Who knows?

A few times he did make it back to the job when the *situations* took over.

He could turn up after a day of being assessed. Learnt his rights, right. A man at the bus stop told him this. Pete, he said I'm Pete. If they ever try to hold you, tell 'em Pete said they can't hold you. Pete sat with his back against the glass of the bus stop, a poster, a car beside his ear. Pete had company, a dozen carrier bags: one read Patient's Belongings and Name on it.

They could not forcibly keep him without holding him under the Mental Health Act. Martin John can repeat the section aloud. (Went to the library, looked it up, like Pete told him to.) Not now, he can't repeat it right now because he is sat at the desk. If you repeat things aloud at the desk it never goes well. You know that. We all know that. Martin John knows that.

He can discharge. He did discharge. He has discharged. Many times has he discharged. To stop him, they'd have to prevent him under the Act. Was he a danger? You never quite knew with Martin John. He was persuasive, solid like a crow who could persuade you he was a crow.

When he returned to work after being discharged the previous day or night—he usually felt better if he discharged, fine just fine—it surprised him he could feel so fine, while some contemplated him close on a danger. Perplexing.
These were his better days.
Those were his better days.
The days he discharged.
The days when he could discharge.

⋯→

Today though is strangely NOT A GOOD DAY. This is unusual. Not doing the best is Martin John. Not a good sign. A sign of change. Martin John is worried.

Tell us why, Martin John. Tell us why.

He's worried about the pile that Dallas has stacked.

I don't like the way they sit. Why would he do it, knowing only that I was on the way in? He did it because he believed I would not and could not make it in. He expected me not to be here this evening for my shift. He expected me never to return. They have given away my job. My job is given away. I have no job. Stop asking me questions. Stop inquiring. You're in on it. You probably told him I was in the hospital last night.

You were in during the day on the short-stay ward, remember? That's right: day, night, what harm is in it?
Plenty harm is in it Martin John.

Plenty harm when the papers are looking at you stacked that way. They've been stacked deliberately that way.

They're sending a message.

I'm getting the message, says Martin John.
I'm fucken getting it, is right.

⋯→

The only thing to do when he's getting the message is to take the message on a walk.

⋯→

He is staring at the papers that Dallas has stacked in a different way and he cannot tackle the rearrangement until he completes a circuit or 17 circuits because today's number is 17.

17 P words is what he read in the morning paper before work. This will require 17 circuits if he is to follow the sequence. He intends to follow the sequence if there are no interruptions. No interruptions by Meddlers. The plague of his life. If there are interruptions there's another plan.

⋯→

The 17 P/p words included a high volume of repetitions of the words political and part. Do your part, he can hear us telling him. Do your part in this story. Everyone wants a story. Everyone has a story. Everyone is a story. He believes we are telling him to do his part, do his political part. He won't be your story. He won't be your political story or the part in your story.

Shut up, would ya. He cautions us.

Over there by the door enters the postman. Normally he wouldn't be troubled by the postman but on account of the arrangement of the words and the P in postman he's keen to avoid him because it's trouble. But he wants a signature for a delivery.

Martin John knows this *ostman is trying to get his signature because they're *robably trying to *rove he's here. He *uts his two hands on his head and *ulls at his scalp. He has to think fast. How fast can you think, Martin John?

Stop, he says again. Stop.

You could scribble your name in a way he cannot read it. We tell him this.

Shut up, he says, knowing we are right.

I can't write, Martin John tells the *ostman.

Fuck off and sign this says the postman.

Martin John signs. I don't know what I've signed, he says to the postman. He fears trouble ahead.

···→

17 words with the letter P today.

Poorest, public, perilous, price, parliament, products, purse, people, partner, pay, people, prices paid, pink, pre-boomtown, paving, powersharing,

There were P words the day Martin John was discharged: pointed people peaceful put prescribing psychiatrist.

Mam warned him about Meddlers. Not exactly. That wasn't it. Mam warned him about getting his photo taken.

That was it.

Precisely.

Be careful. Duck. Don't ever let them take a photo of you. Someone might see it. Someone from home could recognize you. They'd come for you and *it*'ll be over.

⋯→

It is never defined.

⋯→

In order to prepare for the Meddlers' attempt to bury him, Martin John has done copious amounts of research to help him understand how they meddle, where and how they'll attack. His research consists of endless hours of videotapes of people speculated on the news. He commenced with cassettes but found them too easy to destroy. He tries for local news programmes where the reports are more detailed and the Meddlers announce themselves.

He's alert to the weapon that is the camera. The spy tube. The eyewitness pry. Any camera hoping to seek him out will fail. He can dodge them with the speed a mugger takes flight. Any camera—whether student-, tourist-, or ITN-operated—and he is gone. He has a ritual for passing by a camera and letting the camera operator know he will not participate. That he is not giving them permission to capture his image.

⋯➔

A Meddler with a camera would be the final clunk-click.
He understands it was a photo that got him into trouble.

⋯➔

Martin John does not like Meddlers.
Meddlers don't understand things can upset a fella and get
him down.
Meddlers can't comprehend this.
It's why they're Meddlers.
You've to be doin' jus' right
jus' right.
You've to be alright.
Full fucking safe right.
Exactly how they want you to be.
Except you've to do their right.

⋯➔

*You've to be prepared Martin John. You've to be ready. You
have put us in this situation mind. I warned you, I had you
warned and you didn't heed me. Not once have you heeded
me, perhaps now with the help of God and the devil's promise
you'll heed me.*

WHAT THEY KNOW:

Rules.

Rules have already been broken in this book. The index told us about refrains, not rules. There was no mention of rules early on. Martin John will not like this.

Meddlers have rules. Rules have Meddlers. Meddlers do not tell you the rules until you've broken or filleted them.

They've rules, Meddlers. Rules none of the rest of us are privy to 'til they tell us. Youse'll do it this way, which is my way, Meddler way. Even if Meddler way is going through the cow's mouth and out its ear to go up its arse, Meddler way prevails. Meddlers prevail at work and it troubles Martin John. He doesn't like Meddler way. Mam doesn't even know about Meddler way. She didn't warn him. She shoulda warned him. She shoulda, he says that aloud so we, who might be sitting nearby, can hear it. We, who might be sitting nearby, find out-loud pronouncements worrying. We pretend the person, in this case Martin John, has said nothing and we stare ahead. Martin John is grateful for our avoidance.

Even if they've no rules Meddlers'll make some up while you are standing there. A Meddler is trouble brewing, trouble half-cooked, trouble that'll come back and bite him in the ear. There's a stoic quality to Meddlers.

Meddlers won't rust in the rain.
Meddlers order off menus.
Martin John does not eat out.
He doesn't trust kitchens.
Fuck the Meddlers.

It was always the Meddlers who interfered and turned him in. It was the Meddlers who turned him in the first time. It's the Meddlers who'll turn him in the next time. It's the Meddlers who'll bury him.

--→

58

His Meddler research, the videotapes, all sit up, tower-wards, in a lifting stack, until they beach at the ceiling, end. There is no abrupt interruption from floor to ceiling. Neat. Precise. Up. Identical. Up. Identical tapes up. Identical red-and-black cases up that give no indication to their contents. No scribbled titles, no scrawled-upon stickers. No blue biro. They separate from the 9 years' worth of Eurovision Song Contest recordings, which rise and archive themselves in the identical manner, along the parallel wall. His cell is walled tapes. His wall is cells of tapes. There is no voluntary wall space unoccupied. No section available. Also, the titles are not labelled. He keeps them stowed. Secret. Un-de-code-able. Martin John has binders full of numbers that correlate to his tapes. He studies the tapes from time to time. More obviously, he studies the streets. He is out walking by day. Watchful.

Inside things are safe. Except for the one big problem.

⋯➔

His best weapon for observing Meddlers is the puddle. He can stand by a puddle and wait for them to pass. He can stand in their way. Just. Like. That. Stop! Stop hard and abrupt in the middle of the pavement. Sometimes people bump into him. He likes that. They apologize. The Meddler will claim not to have seen him. They call him mate. Instead of bait. He is bait. Baited to them. But subtracted now because of a puddle. A puddle is the most successful way to separate from a Meddler.

All Meddlers and the noticeable increase in Meddlers can be traced to the arrival of Baldy Conscience. There have always been Meddlers but never ever at this volume. It was Baldy Conscience who brought the maximum Meddlers out.

He has a prepared statement to deflect them. He raises his hands carefully in front of his eyes and repeats, "I don't contribute, I don't contribute to these things." He takes no chances since the advent of palm-held video cameras, which are regularly found on Tower Bridge Road in the hands of Italian tourists. No distinction is practiced. He practices no distinction: if it is a camera, he performs his declaration. It matters not who possesses the camera because as his mother has long told him *you just don't know in whose hands these things might end up*.

⋯→

A photo has put him in the situation with Baldy Conscience, he must remember this. He must not have a camera near him. Ever. No cameras ever. No women ever. No Meddlers ever.

⋯→

All photos have been removed and burned. If they come they will find no photos.

⋯→

If Ralph says he gave him the picture Martin John will say No picture. Never no picture.

⋯→

Mam warned him about getting his picture taken.

Be careful, she said. Duck. Don't ever let them take a picture of you. Someone from home might recognize you. They could come for you and *it* would be over.

It is never defined.

With the help of God or no God—Martin John finds it unlikely any God would take pity on a man such as he—he continues not to heed her. These days, instead, he heeds the Meddlers.

The Meddlers I have no choice over, he has told mam. They're not just coming for me, they're here, gunning for me, stamping all over my head as I speak to you. They will get to me before the guards. I'll be dead before the guards come for me.

Whenever Martin John talks of the Meddlers she drills him for information and—should he spew any small bit—disputes and dismisses it. So he has begun to withhold the information, but he's withholding it in the only way he's ever managed to withhold anything from his mam—a wriggling withhold. I wouldn't tell you for it would put the fear of God in you and we wouldn't want that. He speaks to her like she is a fragile imbecile. She gets cross, demands to know what he is waffling about. *Make sense would you, make sense before I come and make sense of you.*

But what is the point, for as soon as Martin John begins detailing the ascent and assailing ways of his nemesis Baldy Conscience, mam retreats into pleading that he *shut up, shut up, shut up. For Christ's sake shut up with this old shit would ya.* And she is back drilling him again on the details of his day and night.

Has he work?
Is he working?
Are you working?
What's he spending his money on?
What time is he home?
Is he getting out to Noanie each week?

61

And most of all: the women—has he been careful? Has he been careful around the women? *We don't want it happening again. It'll be over for you if you slip again.* And she finishes with the promise it's prison he'll be and she's closing the line now and so he should think careful. *I'll hand you over, I'll tell them all—you've given me no choice.*

She is usually saying this as the pips on the line declare his money is gone. Pip. Pip, pip, pip. Dead.

--->

Harm was done.
Harm was done and further harm would be done.

He had done *it* before, but he never did *it* again.
This is what he tells them.
The ones who ask.
Like mam.

*When they come for you Martin John it's at night. They wait
'til they know you're home. Then they swoop. They want to
bring you out quiet and without a fuss. Go quiet and without
a fuss. All they want to know is they've got you. They want to
say they have you.*
They never come for you at work.
If you're at work they can't get you. Say it aloud now.

If I am at work, they can't get me.
(Martin John repeats.)

Nights. It only happens on the night shift. Martin John, his torch for company and his stride. His seat, cheap soup and cold thermos that sometimes leaks. He has the station, it's all his and he's safe. The threats are to a building that he is in and they could get him, but they won't. One of the reasons he works nights is because if they are going to come for him, he figures it will be at night and he won't be home to be lifted.

It has to be difficult for them to come for him. To find him. If it's difficult they'll go for someone else. He gives the daylight a wide berth. Mam told him it is only at night they come for you. They're too busy with other criminals during the daylight to be bothered. But it's at night they grow curious about the like of you, the ones who they cannot be sure have done *it* or not.

Martin John understands perfectly what she is not saying in what she's saying. She's saying that night is when they review the tapes. The tapes that they have been taking of him all day long.

⋯→

Night was the time the funny stuff happened with Martin John.

Night was the time when he felt her wrath more keenly.

She had strong rules about night. She said they would have to show darkness in the house at all times or suspicion would be attracted. She said they must act ordinary. She said people did it during the Blitz. They couldn't risk a knock at the door. No inquiry Martin John, she said. We don't want to encourage it. It made everything harder, her obsession with not encouraging inquiry. *It* was never defined. Every single action they undertook (once he had fouled things up) was completed under the jurisdiction of *not attracting inquiry.* Shopping would be done far from the nearest town. Necessity. A seized state of forced normality prevailed. Perspicacity. However, she made choices that did attract attention. She (sometimes) kept him from school. He (simply) disappeared from the system. It was as though she thought they'd fail to notice.

...→

Who knew? He knew. He knows he knew but did you know?

At night, after the incident or that incident, for there were more incidents than she knew about, she locked him in his room.

He was a danger to himself and her and it was for the best that she lock him in.

So she locked him in.

In she locked him.

You'd have locked him in.

Until she could get him out of the country. She'd to get him out.

There was the matter of the bathroom. She never addressed it. He learnt to use the bucket. He learnt to wait for morning to come. Sometimes it came and she didn't always unlock him early. Once she forgot him 'til 11 am. She said sorry. She said he needed rest. She said Get down now, duck! Because the postman was at the window. She said there were no eggs. That day she said a lot all at once and Martin John was dizzy.

...→

They're closing in on you, she told him, Friday's the day will do for us. We've to get you out. Now she no longer asked him what he had done. She would not touch *it*.

No, she said nothing other than get down and we've to get you out.

⋯→

Not long 'til she planned his exit.
Not long 'til she planned his exit then.
We've to get you out.
That's how it was.
She said they'd left it too long. She did not ask him whether he'd done *it* anymore.
Only that *it* could have been a misunderstanding and he could have apologized but they'd left it too long and they were coming for him.
I'll try, she said. I'll try to save you.
I think I know the kind of girl she is.

WHAT THEY DON'T KNOW:

He has made mistakes.

Martin John has made mistakes. He went exactly where mam said. He did as he was told.

Except the small, crampy house in London. She does not know about the crampy house. He minded it. Well it was another fella's. Ralph's. But him gone "away" to prison. They met briefly. Martin John was the landlord now. Sorta.

···→

He shouldn't have because if she knew she'd explode. He minded the house from back before the new trouble started. It was a sort of borrowing arrangement. A man in a spot of bother who needed his rent paid and eventually he'd come back once his bother was spotted. Because Martin John had a clockwork pay packet he got it and managed to hang onto it, with a few close blips on the rent radar. Located in a handy but grungy location, it was a cereal-box house with butter-dish-sized rooms and a kitchen not much bigger than a school locker.

···→

Periodically Martin John rents to Lithuanian cleaners or Danish students or Polish taxi drivers and this is dangerous. He tried to find the quiet ones who don't proffer information, don't wash so often and won't boil the kettle dry.

He prefers the ones who don't stay long—especially the illegals. He can tell them when they ring the bell because they dress smarter than needs be, but their socks and shoes never match and they have a jittery look about them. He always offered the room to an illegal first. They don't realize they're getting it because they won't stay.

The Spanish?

Never!

Too fond of the night and too heavy on the floor above his head.

A Brazilian? Yes!

Rosalie, her lips were incredible—no woman should be bestowed lips that beautiful was his first thought. He almost didn't give it to her because of the lips: they'd be a distraction to the business of his day. He regretted Rosalie because she still wrote and there was that time he had to go to Heathrow to the Immigration and swear blind she was his and she said she'd never forget what he did, and he wished she would forget because she still writes, though he replies infrequent. The Christmas card he allows her. The card he allows them all. Signed only with his surname Gaffney and MJ dashed after like he's the single Gaffney there is. (The tin of biscuits at Christmas, that he ceased because he did not want tenants needing to speak to him such as to say Thank you.)

No nationality has permission to knock on his bedroom door. Ever.

They could leave correspondence in an old dustpan screwed upright to the left of his door frame. They never complain. He encourages them to report repairs knowing they never will. They were told never knock at the door, leave a note, the pan was ever empty. It's why he liked the illegals. They don't dare ask.

He knows how they think, how they feel, because they always think someone is coming for them, like he does.

He has made mistakes.

There was one (recently) who slipped by him. A Lithuanian or an Estonian—he can't tell the difference between the Baltic states. She wanted to be caught because she left the tablet bottles in the bin and gradually the volume of them made him suspicious. Against his better judgment, which is not to be involved, never to inquire for inquiry leads to involvement, involvement leads to questions and mam has warned him of that.

Stay out of it Martin John, for the love of God stay out of it, I cannot save you now you're in London, get yourself into bed early and stay out of it. D'ya hear?

The day he made the mistake, she, the renter, was unnaturally quiet, so Martin John gave in to curiosity. Up he went, contemplated briefly that he ought to put carpet on the stairs because it's irritating. It's irritating to hear them, the tenants, climbing around him and today he didn't hear her and that was irritating too. That was why he was up to make this inquiry. An inquiry he would later regret. Maybe she could hear him climbing, he doesn't want to be heard, he didn't want to be climbing, but he was climbing and this was not what he should be doing. Knocked. No answer. Retreat to kitchen. A cup of tea drank, three minutes marked on the clock and the decision to check one more time before he left to his late shift.

This time, door tried and it opened. She wanted someone to come in. He continued knocking as he pushed it. She was sleeping.

Sorry now.

No reply, no movement.

He put his hand on the cover and her leg but couldn't wake her. He put his hand up and down her leg considerably longer than was needed to ascertain anything. Furious, more than concerned she might be dead, he placed a 999

72

call on the coin phone, up there, beside the door, stoic and informative. The way the ambulance men looked at him confirmed what mam said. It didn't do for a man of his vintage to be renting to a young woman like that. He finally understood the potency of the word allegation.

I couldn't wake her was the only information he provided. Her name, obviously, did not match any papers about her room and no, he could tell them little about her. *I only rent to them, I am not involved with them. They've no reason or need to tell me anything and I don't encourage it.* When the ambulance men packed her and her stretcher into the van, they inquired if he was to ride with them. *No, he'll wait.* Should he say she was not his relative? Did he already say? What is it they're thinking about him? Do they think he did this to her?

I must phone her family. He offered this blank. After they left he watched a video and waited for the phone call. No call. On account of the look the ambulance men gave him he went to visit her. He walked to St Thomas's where they had taken her and all along the walk mumbled *stay out, stay out, stay out of it for the love of God Martin John stay out of it.*

⋯➤

He phoned all right.

Outside St Thomas's Hospital he phoned.

He phoned mam.

—I only put my hand on her and she was cold, he stuttered.

What have you done Martin John? What have you done? Oh not again, the Lord save us not again.

—No, not again, not again. He repeated. I only put my hand on her and she was cold. I didn't do *it*. I don't remember the moments before or after. I didn't hear her say anything. I didn't do *it*. I was only covering her leg.

He has made mistakes. All his life he has made mistakes. He continues to make mistakes. By Christ if he could only stop with the mistakes.

The hospital was a mistake.
The hospital came after the phone calls.
The hospital was a mistake.
The hospital that came after the phone calls was a mistake.

⸺▸

Ah, he knows the hospital system well does Martin John. In and out. Oh God he does. The way he is himself. The social worker will be called and will be talking to the girl and he's to be ready now, must have the old thoughts in order. He has it in his head now, present like a friend, say little to them and they'll be none the wiser. He's worried about the social Meddlers as he calls them—the social workers—he cannot have them put the Estonian, who may not be an Estonian, in the notebook (as he calls it). He has it now. He has fouled up, he knows it, but he has it in his head now. Up there installed. Beside his mistakes.

Do everything you can to keep the Estonian out of the notebook. Do everything you can to keep the social workers back. Do everything you can Martin John. Do everything you can.

⸺▸

Only the Estonian is miffed at him for delivering her over to them. The Estonian who might be a Latvian is disappointed in him. It is in her eyes as he hands over a box of Roses chocolates, having considered Quality Street too garish for the occasion. Roses were right, he thought. Were Roses right?

—Why did you call them? A plain inquiry in her crickle-crackle accent.

Was she angry because of the Roses or because of him saving her life? Did it matter? He gave her his copy of today's paper, The *Financial Times*, adding he'd like to get it back from her once she's finished. No rush, he put his two palms up. I've done the crossword. She asks in her broken English if he can bring her a magazine tomorrow.

He had no intention of visiting her tomorrow for it would draw further attention to him. This magazine is going to be a problem.

Whether she was angry and about what she was angry faded to interest him. He was angry. She had cluttered up the bin. Thoughtless. He only emptied it every few weeks. Given him strife with the two ambulance men. He thought of mam. He could hear her. He could hear what she'd say. *She's taking the roof down from over you one slate at a time. She'd talk about the greyhound track. She'd talk about the depravity of the country.* She'd talk. That was the problem with mam. Mam talked and he couldn't stop hearing her. Yet could he heed her? No he couldn't. He could not.

Mam'd tell him. She'd tell him alright. *Martin John, what is a man like you, a man with an allegation, doing near a woman like that? They're out there Martin John, waiting for you, they want to trip you and they want you to trip. You're a fool. You've to be onto them. You've got to get ahead of them. D'ya hear?*

Mam called him a man with an allegation. He was a man with an allegation. But there was more than one. The others were not out loud yet. But they could come out and if they came out, well then they'd come for him. That's how it is Martin John, that's how it is when you're a man with an allegation.

He knew what to do.

When the time was right he'd let her go. How many days out of the hospital could he leave it, before telling the Estonian she'll have to move out? If a woman tried to top herself above you on a single divan how many days might you give her before you told her she had to go? Should he tell her now, here in the hospital? Could he whisper it over to her or put a note in the magazine she'd requested? He didn't know. He didn't have the answer to this question.

He returned with a magazine and handed it to the nurse who, confused by the instruction could she keep it from the girl 'til tomorrow, tsks there's no need for that, I'll take it over straight away (and obviously intends to deliver it straight to the girl in a we'll-say-no-more-about-it practical manner).

He must now return and visit her tomorrow, a move abjectly necessary because of the predicament this young one has thrown at him. Because of the way the nurse has looked at him.

···→

Two days after she was discharged from the hospital he told the Estonian his sister needed the room. The sister who was married in Beirut? She asked. No, he said, another sister altogether. She was on her way from Ireland and needed the room for a few months. A pregnant sister. A pregnant sister in trouble needed the room.

76

The Estonian appeared not to hear him correctly, so he repeated: two weeks, if she could find herself another arrangement in two weeks it would be best for the pair of them. A house where there would be someone to keep an eye on her. She cried. He exited to eat a pork pie. When he returned she was still red-eyed.

—Do you mind, she said, do you mind to bring me to the bus stop? I am confused. I don't remember where it is.

He pulled on his old coat and as he walked with her, she held his arm tight. Past them, the cars mutated into each other, a noisy blur that put paid to the obvious silence. He stood beside her like a leek, counting to 40 and preparing to excuse himself.

—There's enough room for all of us, she stated as the bus approached. He resisted the urge to ask about Russia's 1984 Eurovision entry.

Mam was right, always right. He was trapped now. She was trapping him. Not even a pregnant sister in trouble could shift. We can share the room, she said before stepping onto the bus.

To be rid of the woman who may be a Latvian, an Estonian or a Lithuanian (he should know them all, from his frantic Eurovision studies, a further failing not lost on him: the first failing he let her in, the second she forced him to visit her in hospital), he sought unofficial help from the Department of Immigration. It was a cruel swipe, a dirty one, but since he hadn't heeded mam's warnings, he had been scalded. He knew precisely what his mam would do.

In the middle of his shift—and thus in the middle of the night—he phones their tip hotline and leaves a description of her and his address. He adds matter of fact that he didn't know was she an Estonian or Latvian or Lithuanian but these were the hours they could find her there. He adds another line about respecting the laws of this country and Glad to be of service, which, when he hangs up, he regrets. He sounds like an MP on *Newsnight*: pious and prompt, while his accent gives his origins away.

⤑

He was unhappy with what he had done. It might have felt right before he did it, but once he'd done it, an overwhelming urge to reverse it hooked him. It was always this way when he made mistakes.

He kept a careful eye out for the immigration people coming for her. He told her he had seen them snooping around. He assured her that he'd do everything to prevent them access.

—You're like my family, she sighed.

—Not at all, he rebuffed.

—You're a very good man, she added.

—I am not, he assured her.

⤑

78

One morning, weeks later, he returns to find her room cleared and she's gone. He's puzzled. It was what he wanted, but now she is gone something is wrong.

There would be no tip line to remove her replacement: Baldy Conscience.

⇢

He has made mistakes:

Martin John has made mistakes.

Baldy Conscience continues to be his biggest mistake. He has been a five-year mistake. A repeated spade-to-the-back-of-his-head mistake. Baldy Conscience lied when moving in. He cannot remember the exact shape of the lies but Baldy Conscience is not who he said he was. He said he was a quiet man. Baldy Conscience said he liked building ships out of matchsticks.

Baldy Conscience was when all the latest trouble officially started again. He is at the bottom of his current situation and he knows it. He even tells the Doctor in the hospital about Baldy Conscience. He fucked everything up for me. I think there's legions of people out there bothered by him. He's probably causing the trouble in Beirut. If you killed him now or tomorrow all would be well. He doesn't smile when he says it. The Doctor looks down at his paper and etches something onto it.

He has made mistakes.
Baldy Conscience was a terrific mistake.
Baldy Conscience was a turbine of a mistake.
He was a tubular bell of a mistake.
A Chernobyl-fucking-cloud of a mistake.

It was a grave error, an awful grave one.

He was swayed by the accent, by the good boots on the young man and the thinning hair on his head. If a young man had boots like those, there couldn't be much up with him.

And he was in. Baldy Conscience was in to his house and it was only on the second day he realized the man had guitars, and there was to be no guitars.

There could be no guitars because where there's a guitar there's people and didn't he tell the fella he could have the room all right, but no visitors? No people coming around. Ever. Did he use the word ever?

He did.

How many fucken ways were there to say No people comin around. Ever.

⋯➔

Baldy Conscience was not an illegal. He hadn't the fear of an illegal. He was fearless. Disgustingly so.

They all want the room as soon as it is advertised because it is cheap and there's nothing cheap in London. He'll have to be shut of him, but how will he get him out? He was not an illegal like the Brazilian and he was not a woman like the Brazilian. All good. All fine. He didn't want any women, nor Brazilians, after that young one pouring pills into herself.

Mam told him, *no Martin John* and *be careful Martin John* and *keep away Martin John* and *for the love of God Martin John, into bed at 9 Martin John, if you're not in the way of trouble you'll not meet it Martin John.*

And he was in the way now. He was well away in the way. He had scored a hat trick of being in the way. Snookered. Scuppered. Sunk. A scattered, sloping skunk.

But the problem of the Baldy Conscience—his guitars, his blokes with guitars who kept coming around—is not away. They were cute all right, cute in the brain, cute hoors they were. They were cute way into tiny dimensions and holes he couldn't locate, with their wiggling an' worming and almighty fucking burning. Of Him. They had him cornered there below them and were torching him. They were pissing on his head up there. They had him all right. Fuck they had him. They had him in ways he couldn't have foreseen it was possible to be had. They wore hats and tight jeans and black boots like disguises.

Knock the front window, not the door, and the window above shook with the house so old and draughty. He could not go out and confront them with: Who are you and why are you at my door? Couldn't go out and yell at the little gobshite that nobody means no-fucking-body, nobody did not mean a young fella with a sackful of guitar. And it was not just the one, they were all the same, only difference was the length of their hair, the bags under their eyes, the depleted heels on their shoes. Do these gobshites not know the shoe repair, the shoe repair on every street and railway station in this confounded city from Baker's Street to Battersea? A man stuck in a hole in the wall with cylindrical machines to resurrect the British shoe and these hairy eejits not willing to shell out two pounds for a repair. This was one of so many things that frustrated Martin John about this hapless young fella and his unwelcome entourage.

Cunt, the Baldy Conscience says cunt. Upstairs on the pay phone he says it. So often he said it. Cunt this and cunt that and he's a cunt and she's a cunt. He doesn't like the word. Cunt makes him think of thunk. The sound his thump made. Martin John doesn't like the word, he doesn't like it at all and he closed his door each time they rang the phone. But still the accent, the gutteral c-c-c and the swallowed unt. Martin John kicked the skirting board when he heard it to be shut of it. But it wouldn't go. There was usually a pile of videos in the way and the pile took the kick and made a clatter. It was a bad word, a bad, bad word, an awful word that made him think of the women and the woman and the girl and he won't think again of the girl because if he remembers that day then he'll go through it in his mind and wonder about where he was. Was he on the edge of the plastic seat as he remembered or was he at the edge of the box beside her, as her mother stated? He can't recall the small of her back. He can recall the thump. The thump he gave her. Sometimes it is there and sometimes it is not. He can see the fabric of her skirt. He remembers the woman at the reception who pointed her finger at him. He remembers where he gave the girl the thump. That is why he doesn't like the word cunt.

But it's what they said Martin John, it's what they've said, and when it's what they've said Martin John, said mam, *there's no way you can change it. There isn't a way it can be changed. It's all over when they've said it. They've said it you see. Now it's said.*

And he remembered now how she negotiated his exit, when he preferred for *it* to go to trial. *Put me up there and I'll tell what happened. But no she said. She said no, no, no Martin John. We'll atone with God, not the law. We'll atone with the man who knows you best.*

Because mam said he hadn't done *it*, right? That's what he heard. Because mam said she knew the kind of girl she was. That's what he heard. Mam knew him too. And that was the reason he hadn't done it. Because mam knows him and tells him what he's done, right? She told him long and wide and repeatedly and never did she say, *you did it Martin John. You're a dirty bastard and you did it.* She hasn't said it. Did you hear her say it?

The Baldy Conscience drives him out of his own house. The house where he is in charge. He is no longer in charge. Baldy Conscience is in charge.

Every time that skanky-headed lute Baldy Conscience uses the cunt word Martin John must immediately walk and let him know he's walking. How he cracked that fucking door closed. Let that signal reach up to them with their amps and pedals penetrating the foundations of his, well, *Ralph's* tiny brick house and them ensconced in his cheap-room-rent with no carpet nor wallpaper and now he'll have that fuckwit in the kitchen in an hour frying sausages for the other fuckwits and it is all too much. Much too much and he was having none of it and yet it is having all of him. It is consuming him.

And Jesus fucking Christ, tonight, tomorrow and the week after as well, the sneering outta that fella would crumble a statue. He had a disgusting way of conducting himself. The way he spoke, the way he thought, the way he looked, there was even something sinister about his breathing. He was possessed. Even beyond the guitar strings, Baldy Conscience was a sight.

As he walked down that road, beneath and between and beside the concrete overpass and down to the Elephant & Castle and past the flats, those endless flats, with their identical boxy window, ditto door and traipsing family of three to five to seven, all their extras weighing down the buggy and the arms and the hair of the women struggling—at every window he cursed. He cursed all who lived behind those windows or any window, for where there were people, he would have problems and he put his two hands over his ears to indicate it should all go away and on he walked 'til he reached the silly pink shopping centre, where food and sofas on tick are to be got and watery tea upstairs and he'll go to the woman by the Tube station entrance in her doorway with her papers and he'll buy two of the same paper and he'll do that crossword sat on a wall, opposite the gospel church, or if it's raining he'll slip inside and kneel and sit back and complete his clues until the pastor comes or the black women clean their church and add a flower to the sagging bunch.

Once he was sat there when the church was hoovered and it was a mighty sound, whoooming around the Lord like that, sucking up the dust like a chorus, in a way that was so out of place it said the Lord had failed, that his house should never get dusty or need a hoover. You've failed! he called out to Him and the cleaning woman came with the polish and cloth in her hand and told him get out, waving the can of polish like she might spray him in the mouth for his disrespect.

Sometimes, when things got very indescribably bad, he fled as far as Euston Station. Euston is his ultimate destination. It is the only site of paradise in the pigeon-shite-soaked, clogged-up drain of a city. The time of the day is what decides it. If Baldy Conscience uses the c-word in the morning, that's shite. As a precaution Martin John wears earplugs inside his own house. This means he never hears the doorbell or the kettle whistle and twice it boils dry and twice Baldy Conscience screamed that he left the kettle boiling, you've left the kettle boiling! except Martin John couldn't hear a word, only the lips on the face are moving in his doorway and his arm is pointing to the kettle, a step down from the hall in the kitchen. Martin John was wearing industrial-strength earplugs. He nodded. Baldy Conscience walked back up the narrow narrow staircase.

While he considered ways to evict Baldy Conscience, he suppressed the urge to do him damage by avoiding standing in the same spot as him. If Baldy Conscience moved to the kitchen Martin John remained in his room. He took out the earplugs only to decipher the movements of the man. He has his routine down. Baldy Conscience rises late, normally at 10 am, takes a piss, makes a cup of tea and then makes for the telephone. The most dangerous time for Martin John is around 10:45 am. When he works days, he's gone.

On days after the night shift he puts the earplugs in and does not leave his room 'til 2 pm by which time Baldy Conscience has left to his cleaning job at the market.

Sometimes this means he cannot obtain his 2 newspapers.

Mam wants him to hurt Baldy Conscience. He can hear her, even with the earplugs in. He can hear her telling him what to do about him. *If it's you or him, Martin John, then for God's sake let it be him, let it be him, take the brush to him, take a stick to him.* He longs to beat Baldy Conscience, to crack him in the brain, perhaps with a cricket bat or an old tennis racket with the square press around it like he's seen at the car boot sales, to drive him out of this house. But he must not and he cannot. Instead he must leave his own house, he must leave his house wearing earplugs.

You'd be amazed how many Kit Kats get eaten at the market. And Jelly Tots are popular too. It's crazed how many people think that everyone smokes B&H. And yet when you clean up, it's Silk Cut Blue all the way to the black-bin-liner.

I found half a pie today. Apple. Someone ate only the top off the pastry. I ate the rest.

These are the kinds of snips Baldy Conscience shared.

Baldy Conscience was his worst mistake, but there were others. Martin John knows that. Things have become very bad since Baldy Conscience.

⋯➔

I've a few good years, he said. I've had a few good years alright. Oh but they're over now. It's finished. My best years were in Beirut. Things were the best for me in Beirut. This is what Martin John told them when they lifted him at Euston.

88

Once mam was more direct with Martin John.
I am glad *it* is finished, she wrote.
I am glad you have stopped.
I am glad you are done with it.

WHAT THEY DON'T KNOW:

The circuits.

Martin John finds value in repetition. He always has. As a child he liked to wander around lampposts in town. It drove his mother mad. It took perpetuity to move him anyplace for he would loop endlessly around every lamppost they passed. Mam could go into a shop and come out and be assured Martin John would still be there doing his lamppost loops.

He takes this repetition to Euston. At Euston Station he does circuits. He walks corner to corner in a square. People look up at the departures board while their suitcases and trolleys interrupt his circuits. If one is interrupted, he prefers to recommence it. This is why he loves Euston. It's an opera with an aria that never ends.

It is concurrently why he is good at his job. Martin John does the most circuits in his job. All the guards know this and encourage him to do fewer circuits. Gary, a guard who does virtually no circuits, pointed out to Martin John he was making the rest of them look shoddy. Martin John agreed he'll do Gary's circuits if Gary does his cleaning. Gary looked blank and pointed out they work opposite shifts. Martin John said that's grand: Gary needs to change shifts. Gary said he doesn't need to change shifts because he has three children he has to take care of at night while his wife works at a factory. What he needs is Martin John to stop doing so many circuits and sit down and watch television instead. It's what all the guards do. He makes this statement a question. You won't be able to keep it up. He makes this statement a warning.

It has been enough years that Martin John knows he can keep it up. Gary has no idea the sorts of things Martin John is used to keeping up nor what he's using to keep it up. He does not comprehend the self-imposed pressures Martin John lives by. If Gary had to live with Baldy Conscience, Gary would realize that the circuits are necessary to survive him.

The only deal I can do with you involves you hurting a man. Martin John says it straight, direct, and stares at Gary when he says it. Gary shakes his head. I really don't get you, he says.

—There is a man living in my house and if you can get rid of him, I will do fewer circuits.

—Throw him out, Gary replies.

This conversation is going nowhere. Conversation with Gary never goes anywhere. His brain is the final bus stop on the route.

⋯➔

Another problem with Martin John's endless contested circuits is that Martin John ignores the cleaning schedule. The cleaning schedule that all the guards are meant to adhere to. The cleaning needs to be done. Martin John does not believe in the cleaning schedule because Baldy Conscience has views on cleaning and each time he puts a mop into a bucket, Baldy Conscience comes to mind. He has solved this problem by trading with the Bosnian. He allows the Bosnian to sleep and does double the loops. The Bosnian wakes at 5 am and does Martin John's cleaning. Martin John does two buildings' worth of walking. The Bosnian does 2 hours' worth of cleaning. A good trade. A co-operative European union. The Irish man, the Bosnian. Understood by both men. In two languages. No argument. Ever.

Except when one is off sick.

The Bosnian appears to manage his circuits. Martin John, however, just ignores the cleaning. This is fine.
Unless it rains.

Given it is South London it regularly rains. As eggs are eaten, so it rains. It is the kind of rain that makes its mark. Especially in the hallways. Rain will fall, Rain will fall, Martin John mutters out the windows to the weather. Rain will fall is his code word for I am screwed. Still he doesn't want to go near the bucket. Still he doesn't want to deal with the bucket. Rain does not send him to the bucket. If he goes near a bucket Baldy Conscience looms and all is ruined. He is reminded what none of them know.

BALDY CONSCIENCE IS AFTER HIM FULL-TIME.
Baldy Conscience wants the house. Baldy Conscience wants to be the landlord.

⋯➔

When Martin John ignores the cleaning, Dallas is waiting. He fills up the forms that say the cleaning was not completed. When Martin John arrives for his shift, Dallas leans over the top railing to greet him with the announcement, pointing to the floor that Martin John is walking upon—
Cleaning wasn't done man. Cleaning wasn't done.

Martin John is always apologetic to Dallas but claims his stock excuse that he became distracted reading the Bible. Dallas then asks, which part has he been reading? Martin John repeats whatever he has read because when Martin John does not want to do the cleaning he reads the Bible knowing that if he has done so, Dallas will tear up the form and they can carry on. (Like good Christian men carry on.)

In anticipation of meddling he also brings Dallas cheap pies. The man is a pussycat in the midst of a pie. The cleaning in this instance can be overcome.

Yet Dallas is not the only guard who objects to Martin John doing the dodge on his cleaning. There's that woman guard. There's the woman guard that none of the men like because she is bigger than them, rounder than them, more careful than them, and all things considered, more frightening than doing the cleaning.

Because none of the men like the woman it is easy to escape her accusations. Let's say Sarah, the woman, or the witch as the men call her, reports Martin John has not done his cleaning. Despite the fact the floor and bathroom on the cleaning list remain uncleaned, despite the overwhelming evidence to support this fact, Martin John can opine to the manager—a man whom they never really see unless there's a problem—that Sarah has a vendetta against him. That she constantly reports on him. She hates me. I don't know what her problem is.

She hates us all, the manager once replied.

Sarah's problem is merely that she wants to do her job properly and she wants the guys to do their jobs properly. The guys have other plans. Sarah does not understand people who do not do their jobs properly. It is a serious business having a job. She doesn't like slackers. Yes she eats too much but it's none of their fucking business. They are not paid to guard the opening to her stomach nor calibrate its contents. She does her job properly. She doesn't understand those who don't. You can see the problem the guys have with Sarah. You can see the problem Sarah has with the guys. The manager is stuck in the middle. He likes that Sarah does her job properly, but agrees with the

95

men she is disgusting for no other reason than they insist she is. The manager does nothing. The men call her that fat bitch. One calls her a slag. Sarah only ever talks about the fact they don't do their job. She doesn't mention their waists, or their wives, or the way they smell. And they do smell. Of course they smell. All men in uniforms, indoors, smell because Sarah has the United Nations sense of smell. Her smell is funded by NASA. They could lock me in a lab and ask me to sniff and I'd be useful, she once told Martin John. Sometimes they forget to flush the staffroom toilet. That bothers her bad. They've stopped doing that because she screams if she comes across it and will stand in the middle of the place and say RIGHT. Fucking Right Now whoever arse put that lump of shit in the staff toilet get it down here now and *get rid of it* before I put your fucking head in there with it.

---→

Martin John can easily find his way around Sarah. (For one, he never ever shits on duty.) Go and check my card, he'll tell her.

Go and check my card in the machine and then check your card in the machine and see how many circuits mine registered yesterday, then we can talk about cleaning.

—My card has nothing to do with cleaning. Your card has nothing to do with cleaning. Cards don't do the cleaning. A fucking mop and bucket does the cleaning.

—Your card never leaves the desk.

—Where my card goes is none of your business.

—Where my mop goes is none of your business.

—It is my business. Look at the state of the fucking floor.

—I cleaned it. Then a man walked on it.

—You are the only fucking man in here at 5 am. She has him at that. This is true.

—Check your card, he repeats. Check your card. Then check my card. I have the most circuits.

She walks away talking to herself. She wonders how she came to be sandwiched this way between a bunch of fucking apes. She threatens him. She threatens him by speaking ahead of herself. She does not turn around and threaten him. There would be no point in that.

—There are no cards, she says. You know there are no fucking cards to check.

⋯→

Everyone knows there is a machine in the office where the cards are rumoured to be checked except no one has ever seen the machine. Nor has anyone seen the cards physically get checked. But it's enough. If the manager says there's a machine in there that checks, they buy it. They believe it. They believe in the machine they have not seen.

There are also technically no cards, but each guard has a badge or someone somewhere convinced someone somewhere that this badge is *the card that the machine checks.*

The manager dissolves the tension among the guards by allowing them to have a small black-and-white telly on the desk. He is giving them the one that his family used in his caravan in Great Yarmouth because he says they recently obtained a colour one.

But he warns them: any disputes over the telly and it will go. Also, any cleaning not done or any circuits not walked and it will go.

For a time, peace reigns, Martin John walks the others' circuits, the others do his cleaning, they watch telly while he is chronically walking.

All is well until all is not well.

When all becomes not well it has nothing to do with the cleaning. It has everything to do with Baldy Conscience.

⋯➔

Mam has warned him the only thing keeping him on the straight is the job.

Mam has repeated the only thing he has going for him is the job.

No matter what he does he should never threaten the job.

The job, she points out, stopped you doing the other stuff. The other stuff no one can save him from.

She speaks of the job in the singular as if it's the only job Martin John will ever get. (He is the The in The Job.) As far as she is concerned it is The Only Job. The only job between him and the manhole. If he goes down he'll never come up.

Get to work, get into bed at a good time and nothing will befall you. Don't threaten it all now. Don't do it. And get out to visit Noanie on a Wednesday, she wrote to him in a letter. The world will fall apart. His world will fall apart if he does not visit Noanie every Wednesday. Mam has registered this calculation with the Office of Evaluations. Every time he is admitted to the hospital there has been an interruption to his consistent Noanie visits. She knows because the only time Noanie ever phones her is if Martin John misses a visit. The next phone call that generally follows is from whichever hospital or police station have picked him up. Mam now makes notes on any phone call from Noanie. She notes the time and the date and she puts it inside an unused teapot on the dresser. One day she will open the teapot. She will pour all those receipts onto the table. She will take Martin John's finger and she will trace his history of *not listening to her* by banging it on top of each receipt four times to match I told you so. Nothing I can do. Can't save you now. Over for you.

...→

WHAT THEY DON'T KNOW:

The perils of living with a Baldy Conscience.

It's true that he's not been at *the other stuff* as far as mam knows or is concerned. This could have something to do with the matter of him living in another country and long being of an adult age, whereby the authorities do not report such things to your mother. Mam does not live with Baldy Conscience.

This is the difference in mam's reckoning and the actual reckoning.

She has not put Baldy Conscience onto the map of reckoning.

Baldy Conscience has taken over the other stuff.

Or has he?

Or is he just noisier?

⋯→

Increasingly, all Martin John's roads lead him back to Baldy Conscience. Increasingly, all Martin John's problems begin and end at Baldy Conscience. When he shares this information finally with mam by phone outside, predictably, reliably, she doesn't take it well.

—Don't mention him again to me. Don't mention him. Whoever he is keep away from him.

—Well I can't do that now can I?

—You can and you will.

—He's upstairs.

—Stop going upstairs.

Before he can fudge a reply, three times mam chimes.

—I don't want to hear it, I don't want to hear it, I don't want to hear it.

What they don't know.

THEY DON'T KNOW THAT BALDY CONSCIENCE IS AFTER HIM FULL-TIME. HE IS ON THE RUN FROM BALDY CONSCIENCE EVEN IN HIS OWN HOME. HE IS ON THE RUN. HE DOESN'T GO UPSTAIRS BECAUSE MAM SAID SHE DIDN'T WANT TO HEAR ANOTHER WORD ABOUT HIM. GARY TOLD HIM TO TELL BALDY CONSCIENCE TO MOVE OUT. THEY DON'T UNDERSTAND BALDY CONSCIENCE—HE WILL NEVER MOVE OUT.

WHAT THEY DON'T KNOW:

Check my card.

It was identical when the police picked him up by the tree with his trousers undone. They asked him, What are you doing with your trousers open by this tree?

Three times he replied:

Check my card. Check my card. Check my card.

⋯➤

Martin John has refrains.
At this moment in his life he has five refrains.
We have already met two of them.

His number three:
Rain will fall.

That was rain.
Did you hear that rain?
This is what Martin John will ask.
Rain will fall was his refrain.
Rain will fall is his third refrain.
The refrain that he used when he knew he was about to do
the thing she said she was glad he was done with.
He wasn't done with *it*.
He did not know when he'd be done with *it*.
He was waiting for the signal. The signal that would come
when he knew he was done with *it*. He wasn't done yet.

⸱⸱⸱→

Mam has refrains.
You've to stop this nonsense.
Give over Martin John.
You'll be the death of me.

⇢

He knew they'd come for him one day.
Mam had said they'd come, hadn't she?
I can't save you. Keep your head down.

Rain will fall. Rain will fall on it.

⇢

In nearly every situation there is a Meddler. Martin John
has noticed this. Sometimes it can be the same Meddler
and sometimes it is a brand new Meddler and sometimes
there's a band of Meddlers. He has learnt to identify them
vocally. His response is to announce *"I don't contribute, I
don't contribute."*
   Hands up, eyes down.
   Stride, stride, stride.

He has a big problem now that a Meddler is inside his
house. A Meddler has been in his house for a long time
and he cannot get him out. He has meddled his way in, as
Meddlers will do. The Meddler might have been sent by
the man who owns this house. A man Martin John should
never have gotten involved with at all. A man who said *no
women*. Or was it mam who said *no women*? A man who'd
sent a man to test him. All men become a man.

All men become the road that leads to Baldy Conscience.
If he had heeded mam, there would be no man.
There would be no Baldy Conscience.
It is too late to heed her.

⋯→

Once Martin John did contribute. He let up and the Meddlers caught him. The Meddlers trapped him, so they did. In a hospital ward he was. Lambeth maybe. Not North London anyway. There weren't enough roundabouts for it to be North London. They picked him up by the flyway. They said he said he was going to fly away onto the flyway. Martin John actually said he planned to kill Baldy Conscience and was waiting to push him onto the flyway.

Why do you think they have chosen me, he asks a couple of people on the ward. They assure him they've no clue what he is on about. But how would they when it is he who has been chosen? If you are chosen you are alone. You are blessed, but mainly you are alone. He has a brief picture of how lonely it must have been to be Jesus or any man chosen for a big book.

He has a new list of situations where being chosen doesn't suit him.
Wedding, having to give your daughter away.
Wedding, having to make a speech.
Moving house. Driving the lorry to move people. To decide where people's sideboards or bunk beds must go inside the van.
Plumber, replacing a U-bend.
Speaking to a visitor on the ward, usually his mother, his only visitor.

WHAT THEY KNOW:

The phone calls.

Was the Eurovision fuss a fuss or a situation?
He's not sure.
It was a fuss and a situation.
A fussy interrupted situation.

He should not have done it and he knew better, but every year the compulsion of the Eurovision came around. Those two weeks he took holidays from work or pulled sickies. He'd eat, breathe and definitely not sleep for his pet The Eurovision Song Contest. He journeyed each day of those annual two weeks to a particular newsagent's, where the man Mr Patel told him to *"take your time, take your time"* going through the newspapers because he knows Martin John'll end up buying them all—nearly 10 quid each day for a week in paper sales.

When interviewed, Mr Patel—the most gentle of souls, arthritis in his left knee—could not credit the fight that took place and the bags of sugar that flew, and the tinned steak and kidney pies that were toppled in that brief five-minute bare-knuckle dust-up over the last copy of the *Daily Express.*

The Eurovision pullout special issue was what unhorsed Martin John and the man with his fingers on it. The ordinary Jim Smith of Clapham, who was never in these parts, only that he was calling to his mother and bringing the paper for her. And when it was something for his mother he'd fight to the last and he socked Martin John as Martin John silently stamped on his foot and tried to rip the paper from his hands. Much *what the fuck* and *mate* and *come on then*? And Mr Patel wasn't sure what they're at, but it was loud and his single, central food shelf was wobbling and people crowded the doorway and the police must be called. As Martin John was dragged away, victoriously clutching the *Daily Express*, Mr Patel defended him.

—He's a good man, I known him for years. Not a violent man. A good man.

Meanwhile, Jim Smith was in the doorway regaling the crowd as to how this fucking lunatic tried to rip his arms out. He had my throat, he gasped. He showed them the scratches. The Irish are savages, one man remarked. Martin John is the victor. He's the victor all the way back to the psychiatric ward and that night he slept, injected, still clutching the *Daily Express* under his armpit, rolled up tight.

The next fuss or situation was a fight in the ward over the television. It's the Eurovision song contest rehearsal and a Jamaican fella and another fella with his leg draped over the arm of his chair in an unbecoming manner have the telly tuned to the football and Martin John is not taking it. Sorry now lads, he waltzes over and switches stations and Jamaica roars and the leg-draper springs from chair to television, while Ireland and Jamaica come to blows and security and nurses invade the frenzy with Jamaica landing a few nice lugs to the Mayo jaw while only sustaining sore toes when Martin John resorts to his best tactic, the heel-to-toe grind. And he's off to have his face repaired, his chart now marked for seclusion. He wails like a baby as they X-ray him. Seclusion means no television. Seclusion means another day's loss of Eurovision coverage. He has notes to make. He has observations to record. He has yet to decide whom he is backing. It could be Yugoslavia or Denmark but he hasn't seen Belgium or the Netherlands. He's worried about Turkey because the newspapers said they were swaying their arms in a whole new way and have never improved on their 1977 entry. Switzerland is wearing a worrying swan skirt. Spain is wearing two more such skirts. Greece he's not backing. Greece has produced a doomed song and it's criminal. The German singer prune-tightened his eyes and contorted his face like he was

113

constipated, which makes Martin John think of bathrooms and Baldy Conscience. The thing that has almighty unsettled Martin John is Ireland is hosting the event and he harbours a deep suspicion of Pat Kenny because his name begins with P. He's anxious about the combination of Pat Kenny and Terry Wogan's voices but it all begins and ends with the P, which is why he puts his fingers in his ears to blot out Portugal.

That night things were terrible for him, the worst he decided. As the hallucinations came and came and never ceased, just more and more of them, he was visited the way he's always visited by her voice in his head.

Get yerself out of there Martin John, get the head down, for God's sake stop with this and put the head down and look at your feet and follow those feet Martin John, would you for the love of God follow them and stop all this nonsense. D'ya hear me now Martin John? I want you to listen and I want you to visit Noanie next Wednesday or so help me God I'll land you Martin John and I'll tear you from the place Martin John. I'll drag you by the collar out of there. I don't know what I have done to deserve this Martin John, but I'll tear you from there and I'll redden your arse before I am a day older.

It's her voice. But it's his head. Always her voice in his head.

He has made mistakes.

The phone calls were a mistake.

He nodded, agreed, signed. Nodded, signed, agreed and they let him go.

After the Eurovision incident, he was calmed.

They let him go, until the telephone calls.

Baldy Conscience drove him to the phone calls. If they'd done the right thing and popped Baldy Conscience into the ward or into a river, the phone calls may never have happened. He might never have lifted the phone. I would not have lifted the phone, he told the police who came for him.

It's not right to blame another man for your own carry-on. That's what mam would say. He can hear her say it, even though he's not sure she ever said *quite* that. He can hear her. He can hear that said.

The fuss over the Eurovision was a mistake.
Nobody liked fuss.
Fuss had put him back in this ward.

It wasn't his fault that the other patient wasn't interested in chatting about the Eurovision. It wasn't his plan that that particular insert about a woman in the circus falling from a hoop high in a tent would be on the six o'clock local news. The other parts were his fault. They were definitely his fault. All of them. All his fault. But not the patient and the hoop. Nor the patient distressed by the hoop story, who did not want to talk about Beirut. Beirut was not on the news. Now he remembers that was where it started.

—Beirut's not on the news, do you see that?

He had told the patient in the chair over there inside the useless room they all sat or became angry in. He had carried on a bit about Beirut and about all the lies that have been told and he was leading up to describing his own joy in Beirut, when that patient started screaming about the hoop, the hoop and that the woman was going to fall from it.

He moved back, put his arms up and said he didn't contribute. *I don't contribute.* I don't contribute was what he said. He left the room with his hands up still, remembering that trouble always started when the television went on.

Rain will fall, he said, Rain will fall. Rain will fall when the television goes on.

Because she was a woman in that room there's bound to be a problem. Whenever he is alone in a room with a woman a problem follows. He waits for the problem to come and follow him. He waits for the knock.

Perhaps they won't come for him any more because they have sent Baldy Conscience to annihilate him slowly?

⸺▸

116

Ah they come for him now in the form of Baldy Conscience, or Barely Conscious as he's begun referring to him. That hoor could be sleeping in his bed. Or smashing his videotapes or pissing in his coffee jar, while he's stuck in this ward with a nearby woman angry about a hoop. That hoop woman is about to cause trouble, he can feel it.

---→

Hoop woman told them he used a cushion to cover up what he was doing to himself with his right hand while she was sitting near him in the common room watching the news. He used a pillow, she said. He had his hand on his John Thomas. He was perving out. I could see it. Trapped! Martin John caught her. Was it a cushion or a pillow? At first it was a cushion, now it's a pillow. She was confused. How can you trust a woman confused about a pillow or a cushion? They banned him from the common room. It was no loss, only a useless room in which they went to sit and be angry with each other.

---→

Outside the ward he started slowly. He hoarded in. He stacked papers high. He closed all in and around himself. He lived on tins. Avoided the cooker and told himself Baldy Conscience was Barely Conscious up there and one day soon he'd die. Martin John would roll him out of the house in a wheelbarrow or a trolley borrowed from Tesco.

He imagined depositing his body in the street.
I'd leave it by the kerb.
Half-on/half-off.

I'd hope someone might run over his legs, sever the bottom half of his body. It would equal only half the trouble he has put me through.

⋯➔

The big struggle is time. Where is time and where was time and how has he lost it? Where did the time go in the places he does not remember being? Where was he at the times he cannot account for? What was he doing? Tell it to them slowly. Tell it to them precisely Martin John. Slow it right down or they'll hop ahead of you. The circuits are the only activity that help him record time. Record it absolutely. Tell you absolutely where he was and what he has done. Now they forbid him or intrude on his circuits, he is having more and more trouble accounting for where he has been and what he has been doing.

With no day shift or night shift or circuits, time has become strange, neither protracted nor squat. Just strained. Strange. Estranged. Estuary ranged. There are days, inside in the room, that because the windows are blacked out, he can't tell you if it is day or night. He can't tell if it's night or day? He can't even tell you how he wants to make this statement.

All part of his plan you see. His plan to starve Baldy Conscience into remission. To see him disintegrate like a flea with no blood to feed upon. But as with all plans progress will be slow and tepid. A Baldy Conscience takes a lot of weathering. They don't wilt easy. Will his inquiry take him to Euston? Oh yes it will. He will walk this inquiry around his favourite station. He will visit the flippy ticket window. He will walk and walk until the answer unto Baldy seeks him. Everything comes when he walks on it. When the circuits are intact. When the letters and the circuits add up to an equal.

...→

We've to get you out, mam said.
It was surrender that sentence.
He was back there again.

Harm was done.
But he liked it.
It was hard to credit that harm could be done when you liked it.
It was hard credit why something you liked could be harmful. Harm was done.
He knows this.

I had it in my mind to do *it* and I did it.
He had a mind to do it and he did it.
That's a fact.

He knows this because people in the psych ward group told him.
They told each other. Not just him. It was the code.
Did they agree it was the code?
He cannot remember if it was officially the code.
The same way they'd tell you it was Monday.
It is Monday.
Harm was done.

←...

They had come for him after the incident outside the SuperValu shop, down the lane with the girl.

They had come for him with the one on the bus.

They had come for him that time with the girl who said he put his hand down the band of her skirt.

The other girl where he put his hand between her legs.

They had come for him.

They were her brothers. It was brothers who usually came. Well their fists mostly.

...→

Inside (t)his London house, they couldn't see him. They couldn't come for him anymore. This is why he locked them out. But they'd sent Baldy Conscience in.

Which one has Baldy Conscience come for him over?

The Estonian? The Ukrainian? The Brazilian? Or the one on the Tube?

...→

The one on the Tube sitting next to him right now.

I had it in my mind to do *it* and I did it, he told the British Transport Police as they carted him away. They were waiting for him at the top of the escalator. Four men. Four policemen. No women. They never sent women for him. He rode up the escalator and sailed into their arms. Except they were not waiting for him and had no idea what he was talking about. Until they did have an idea what he was talking about and chased him all around Euston Station. Technically, he said, I've already reported to you. I've done it twice today. It took two of you to come for me. Two of you 'til you heeded me. That's a fact.

⋯➔

He had been arrested for sitting at the top of the escalator and refusing to shift until they removed him. The first few people had said excuse me, excuse me, stepped over and around him until they arrived with suitcases. These had to be lifted over his head.

Finally though it was a woman with a buggy who raised hell. Get out of my fucking way, she said. I mean it, get the fuck outta my way. He didn't budge but the police arrived. His old nemesis the British Transport Police who took so long to arrive despite the "transport" in their name.

I had it in my mind to do *it* and I did it, spoken again as they dragged him away.

Martin John has refrains.
His fifth refrain.

It put me in the Chair.
This is his number five.

⋯➔

It can be a he, she or they situation. A situation did not put
him in the Chair. A collection of situations did. A collection of situations caused by she's and he's and sometimes
even them's. That's not true, mam put him in the Chair.

Things outside himself. He has no control. Mostly it
was a *she* that put him in the Chair. She put me in the
Chair, he would bleat to the doctors.

Perhaps he gave her the idea for the Chair?

The Index does not tell us whether we will know how she
conceived of the idea to put him in the Chair. We will not
be told with whom she conceived Martin John. It's none
of your business, she'd reply to both them questions. (That
would be a *them* situation. *Them* asking what's not *theirs*
to know.)

⋯➔

(From the doctor's notes:)
The patient believes external forces are putting him "in the
chair."

⋯➔

There are whispers. Three times a whisper. What they don't
know, what they know and what they can't know because
Martin John doesn't tell them

He is whispering now. You may find it hard to hear him. Lean in. Try to breathe quietly. You may kick the leaves between the whispers.

What Martin John doesn't tell the doctors, doesn't tell mam, doesn't tell a soulful sinner, wouldn't tell you, except for this Meddler letting you know, is his knowledge Baldy Conscience is after him FULL-TIME, OVERTIME AND DOUBLE TIME. The man is dedicating his life to humiliating and eviscerating Martin John. He must patrol his home, as well as his work, from which he is presently barred, but this has not deterred his patrols. Security will report on the presence of the non-desired former security guard. You can suspend him, tell him he has no job, but you cannot stop Martin John from patrolling. HE MUST GIVE THEM SOMETHING TO DO. HE MUST BE ALERT. The moment Baldy Conscience has plotted will unroll. He is determined to be a witness to this plot. THE MAN IS COMING FOR HIM. THE MAN IS HERE. ALMOST.

⋯➔

He put me in the Chair, he will eventually tell them when they find him. He will be pointing upwards at the roof when he says it. What will follow is howling protest about the pain in his knee as the firemen try to lift him.

⋯➔

Technically it was mam who gave him a full bladder.
The full bladder thing. That pressure thing.
The pressure from the full bladder thing.
That full bladder pressure that he liked the sensation of.
That he never wanted to empty.
That becomes a sexual turn-on.
That forces him to walk even more circuits on the job.
The actual reason he is walking circuits.
To avoid going to the toilet.
To keep his bladder full.
His bricked up bubble.
Right above his exit hose.

The power in the discipline that such control provided: the agony and high of harbour. Every twinge. Each pressure a pleasure. Each demand he piss—refused. Sent to the back of the line. Then, when he eventually did piss—it wouldn't come out. Gah the beauty in that! His bladder's refusal to perform until finally it gave way to an aaah. Sometimes when it would not come out, he would hold it longer. If he could have held 'til it came back up his throat, he would have tried.

After came cramps. He welcomed them. Like he had boiled the pan dry and waited to hear crackled confirmation.

⋯→

IF MAM TOLD HIM TO DO IT
IT WAS RIGHT
RIGHT?

⋯➔

He was forever not listening to her. He had failed to latch.
She told him that. You didn't latch on then and you don't
latch on now.
Now he had listened.
STOP going upstairs, she said.
She was right.
He liked his bladder full.
Steaming full. Ah Ah Ah Full. Up that hill full. Further
full. Further. Further. Further.

His bladder would be plenty full if he never went upstairs.
If he never went upstairs then he never went to the toilet.
Eventually he would have to let it out because of the other
thing, but even the other thing can be kept at bay he has
discovered.

⤏

You know, the fella at work said.

You know, the fella at work who had just caught Martin John with his pants down to his ankles claiming he'd spilled a bottle of HP sauce on them said.

You know, the fella at work, who returned to the toilet, claiming he'd left an umbrella said.

—That's a serious spill. How did it happen? I'm keen to avoid it.

The man is seeking an explanation as to why he, not five minutes ago, found Martin John with his trousers not just down, but very, very down with his dangles *dehors* the usual standard Y-fronts that housed them.

It's drying out, Martin John had said calmly. I have to keep it out until it's dry. Once it is dry I will pack it all back up.

—You know, the man said, I don't understand how it soaked all the way through to your skin when there is a double layer of cloth. He is indicating Martin John's hands, which surround-pound his member and make little effort in the supposed quest of mopping up a complete absence of any sauce spill whatsoever.

Umbrella man was lying. Umbrella man was digging. A digger. Martin John knew the signals. What none of this lot knew was he was living with Baldy Conscience, the sneakiest pig on this earth, so there was nothing that could travel past Martin John. He was Baldy Conscience trained. BC Certified. He wasn't fooled. This was no Innocent Inquiry. It was in his arse. He was angry. Rain will fall, he told himself.

Rain will fall was what he said when he was angry. Rain will fall, he told the fella.

He, misplaced umbrella man, moved away with a look that Martin John trusted even less. Rain will fall, Martin John shouted after him.

⋯➔

I was in the men's toilet, how would Sarah have seen me so? Is she there often? How would she imagine she'd come upon me if she had to go in and clean? We never work the same shifts.

In reply to the question by the Manager fella, Martin John assured him he was not in the habit of spilling a bottle of sauce on himself, so it was unlikely to be a regular occurrence.

But, he added, in the event the Manager fella might be having concerns about him, what would the Manager fella propose he, Martin John, do if, say, his access to bathing facilities was temporarily or for a period of time unavailable? Such as was the case in this circumstance.

The Manager fella would go to the sports centre. London is full of them. Look at the state of people after they play squash. Martin John has his answer and his solution and would hold the Manager fella in ever-rising regard. The man was a ringmaster of solution.

He could see him (the Manager fella) lassoing Baldy Conscience and making him ride stood up on a horse 'til his face turned green and his eyes popped as he surrendered Martin John's front door keys. He imagined eating Christmas dinner with the Manager fella and his family. He felt they understood each other. The Manager fella clattered him on the back and reminded Martin John he was the most punctual person who'd ever worked for him, but there was only so much he could turn a blind eye to. Martin John assured him militarily that whatever had concerned him would only get worse. There was a blank pause where both men nodded and neither man addressed the puzzling adjective. It went the way such meetings always went. For Martin John, any new information, even if it were robust criticism, was a victory. For the Manager fella, worried Martin John was increasingly unhinged, but still he appreciated a reliable worker. Plus the woman who complained about this Irish man also complained about every other man in the place. It was a mistake to hire a woman in these circumstances, but the equal opportunities person had rung and threatened she'd turn his twisties if he didn't do something about the sorrowful state of the workforce on that site. He had deliberately hired the fattest woman he could find because he felt fat women were the right people to sort out problems. It had proven true. He now realized he was a manager who did not want to sort out problems. Just wanted staff to behave so he could be at home by 8 pm and the phone would not keep ringing.

⋯→

For a week things were calmer.

The full bladder thing forces Martin John to walk even more circuits on the job. The only way to ascertain it's truly full is to walk and live that pressure from above.

The original reason for the circuits now has a double purpose.

⋯→

Each circuit would arouse him more and more.
Until he'd "Bucket It."
Now with the full bladder and the increased circuits he is sexually higher than he has ever been.
Thanks to mam.
Thanks to not going upstairs.
Thanks to not being able to use the lavatory.
Thanks to avoiding Baldy Conscience.

⟶

They caught him.
She caught him.
Sarah caught him.
Called his name.
Followed by:
For fuck's sake.
He turned, trousers down.
He could have pulled them up. He had the choice. Could
have pulled them up. Could have pretended he was look-
ing for something in that bucket.
But no. He turned, trousers descended, defiant.
Enjoyed it.

SUSPENDED FROM JOB PENDING INVESTIGATION.

⟶

Check my card was all he said, when she screamed at the
sight of him.
It was in the report. Typed out as her testimony.

⟶

Sarah said she did not wish to say out loud what she had
seen Martin John doing up in the rafters of the building
where they both worked. She said for private religious reasons (all security guards resort to religion when trouble
brews) it would pain her to use the language required.
    First she said private.
    Second she said religious.
    Third she combined the two.
    Doubled her conviction.

Martin John maintained he was caught short and innocently piddling into a bucket that happened to be lurking under the roof beam up there. He claimed a bent kidney. The Manager fella said he'd never mentioned any bent kidney. Martin John agreed and said Ya, right you are, he had no bad kidney. He was just "caught short." The Manager fella looked puzzled by the admission.

Sarah said this is some high tale and he should tell the truth of what he was doing. Martin John said the woman had a vendetta against him and she needed to drop it. Check my card, Check my card, he added.

Nobody ever understands Martin John's instruction to check his card. They usually ignore it. If they asked to check his card, Martin John would present an expired Travel Card. All parties will examine it blankly and this is the most likely reason nobody asks him to expand on the demand to Check My Card.

The card that he is actually referring to is the card he believes registers his circuits of the building. The card he is confused about. Is it deliberate, this confusion? He knows there are cameras. He knows they are spying on him. He knows Baldy Conscience has likely made contact with the people behind the cameras. He likes to make this easier for them, by tapping his Travel Card on the light switch of every floor.

He is not truly sure if those behind the cameras are his employers, yet he does believe in the rumoured machine in the office that they are never allowed to enter. This rumoured machine, which logs all of their movements. The machine that primarily Martin John has rumoured. The threat of the rumoured machine that records what the manager cannot see. Martin John has become so confused about what is where and who is watching him that from the moment he lifts his head off the pillow, he understands he is being watched. This is why he knows that the many times he does the thing to the women's legs and feet or has his trousers undone and *it* out he will be seen. He has told himself he is doing these things to register to them that HE KNOWS THEY ARE WATCHING HIM. I'll give them something to look at, these bread-stealing fuckers. This is partly how he resolves what he's doing. I am letting them know I know they are watching. I know that Baldy Conscience has been sent.

⸺➔

This doesn't explain to him or any of us why he has a history of doing these things. A history that began before Baldy Conscience and a history that commenced before he had any notion of "the trackers" and "their tracking."

This falls into Harm Was Done over Check My Card.

When Martin John admits harm was done, when that refrain circles his mental turntable, it can cause him pause.

The pause quickly fills with self-appeasement. *I had an opportunity. I coulda taken full advantage of the Estonian when she was up there. She was up there waiting on me. She wanted me in a way none of the others did. She offered herself to me and I didn't touch. Well not entirely. I touched a bit. Same as any man would. I took her to the hospital, I bought her a magazine, I took her home. I nodded.*

⋯→

Sort of. But not exactly. There had been some time before he called the ambulance. He had cleaned her up after he had delivered on her. He had cleaned himself up. He remembers clearly the upward strokes with the bunched-up toilet paper. Wipe. Swipe. Wipe. Swipe. Afterwards he worried. Was there a smell? Did the ambulance men suspect something? He thought maybe they might. But he'd checked her pulse and had been quick about it. How quick had he been? He noticed a stain on the roof while wanking over her and made note to check the loft for leaks. He had made himself come by repeating the words jammy jank, jammy jank, jammy jank. He worried now. He had rolled her over facedown to be relieved of her eyes, lifted her dress, yanked down her tights and faded knickers to give him bare bum to toss over. He knew this because he kept one hand pushing resistance against her skin, propping himself over her and his arm had protested his own weight, which only intensified his primary pull. Was she still facedown when the ambulance men arrived? He was worried now. But she had come back, she had returned to the house into the room. She didn't want to leave. He had forced her out. Had she not wished to leave because she liked it? He would never know. Did she know what he'd done? She must have known. She must have liked it. That was it. That was that.

⋯→

Mam does not like the talk about Beirut. She has made this very, very clear. Abundantly transparent. She has told him not to mention the place again. You have never been there, she has been heard to say. Very loud. Very frustrated. Very angry.

135

You've never been anywhere, except Noanie's!
She is wrong.
Martin John has been to Beirut.

He just can't prove it. The way they can't prove anything about him either. They just know what they know and he knows what he knows and what he knows is he believes he has been to Beirut.

...→

The Manager fella sat between the two of them stated he was not present and therefore reliant on witness statements and repeatedly queried the two of them in rotation as to the activity that Sarah saw and that Martin John insisted she could not have seen.

Sarah requested to speak alone to the manager.

She expressed to him what she had seen.

Martin John was suspended from work for two weeks. It suited him as he was behind on collating his Eurovision files.

Sarah was triumphant.

Martin John was more triumphant.

There's misery in triumph, thought Dallas, having endured the dual carriageway of bickering in each direction.

⋯➔

—I have a confession to make, Martin John eventually said to the Manager fella.

—Right.

—I was having a problem, but it is all finished with now.

—Right.

Martin John did not expand on the problem. The Manager fella repeated the word Right. It ended the way these conversations always ended between the two of them. The Manager fella reminding him he was the most reliable person who worked for him and Martin John maintaining he took great pride in doing a good job.

⋯➔

Martin John again to the Manager fella.

—Could I have a word?

—Yes.

—I was having a problem, a medical problem.

—Right.

—I was having a problem like you know, *going*.

—Right.

—So that was how I was caught short.

—Right.
—It is fixed.
—Right.

Martin John supplied no further details. The Manager fella said Right one more time. His phone rang. He disappeared. He returned. Martin John made no further effort to converse, choosing to announce he was due a circuit and wouldn't want to get behind.

He left with his pretend swipe card, faster than the Manager fella could express confusion or muddle out words such as What exactly are you on about?

Martin John realized on the 23rd floor that the Manager fella had returned to speak to him after the phone rang. He interrupted his circuit to go and find the man. Arrived at the 13th floor on foot and changed his mind. He climbed the stairs again to the 23rd floor repeating the words Rain will fall, Rain will fall, at the summit of every floor ascended.

⋯→

Complaints were subsequently raised about Martin John's personal hygiene. Martin John maintains poor hygiene because he wants the putrid smell off him to drive Baldy from his house. If he smells bad enough, the man will have to up and leave. This olfactory battle strategy seeps into his day job where smells trail him and oust him there.

Because Martin John had worked 7 days that week, including one double shift, the Manager fella did not pass along the complaints to him. Instead he did what the dentist does and put a watch on the tooth.

⋯→

Martin John observes the Manager fella leaving the office much more than usual. Each time the Manager fella approaches the guard's desk, Martin John—never doing anything more illegal or illicit than reading the Bible to keep Dallas happy—brightly tells the Manager fella that Rain will fall.

Rain will fall, he'll announce even when rain is indeed falling and has been falling for the past 7 hours. His choice of the same statement troubles the Manager fella, who is actively patrolling for signs of poor body scent. Martin John is onto him. And onto them. And onto talcum powder. Lily of the Valley. Every orifice dusted with the stuff. Shoes lined with it. He is springing lily puffs, if he moves swift. Martin John is onto them. He even pats a layer of it into his underpants.

The thing none of them factor in is the thing none of them know.

THEY DON'T KNOW THAT BALDY CONSCIENCE IS AFTER HIM FULL-TIME. He is on the run from Baldy Conscience even in his own home. Baldy Conscience wants to be the landlord. He doesn't go upstairs because mam said she didn't want to hear another word about him upstairs. Gary told him to tell Baldy Conscience to move out. They don't understand Baldy Conscience. He will never move out. The earth could stop spinning. It could turn upside down and that fucking flump will remain at his kitchen table.

This is why he has stopped washing.

This is why he is holding in his urine.

The plain person cannot understand the punishing details of what the random man who has Baldy Conscience AFTER HIM must endure.

Martin John comforts himself with the prospect that Baldy will ever be after someone, someplace, thus any man or woman who scorned or doubted Martin John was a mere spot behind him in the queue. I'm keeping the fucking seat warm, he would tell them if pressed. It's a fucking charitable act. This man would have his hands around your neck if he did not already, metaphorically speaking, have his hands kept busy around mine. You understand me now?

All Martin John's sentences start terminating with *you understand me now*? If he's buying a ticket or asking the time or even saying hello he leaves nothing to false interpretation. Occasionally a person will respond that, in fact, they *do not* understand him. He will nod a few times and immediately make haste. It indicates Baldy's gotten to them. They're tainted. Stained with Baldy's stump if you like.

140

He has made mistakes
Baldy Conscience was a terrific mistake.
He was a blood clot of a mistake.

On account of Baldy Conscience
He only rented if he had to.
He only rented if he had to.

On account of Baldy Conscience
He only rented if he had to.

No more women.
No more women.
There would be no more women.
This was how Baldy Conscience slipped by him.

He preferred the upstairs empty with the windows wide open. Rooms free: life good. He shut them only if he used the telephone, after which they would be promptly opened again. In the empty rooms he walked in circles. Sometimes he just stared at their ceilings. A negotiation between him and the plaster: Do you see you are empty? You are empty because I have made you that way.

When things were going grand:
The upstairs rooms were empty.
Each day he followed his rituals on time.
Letters and circuits matched as they should.
His walks were a pleasure.
The newsagent had his papers.
The pork pie did not leave a greasy taste on the roof of his mouth. His urges stayed quelled. Hidden deep under a mental duvet.

He knew things would be grand if he put his head down, kept to himself and stayed in at night as she had told him to. Then they would not come for him because there was nothing to come for.

When things were bad he felt they were coming for him. He felt it every minute of any day when things were bad.

WHAT THEY DON'T KNOW:

Martin John wants to touch your leg.

Whenever things sour down on the job Martin John heads to Euston.

Whenever Martin John is anxious about going home to face Baldy Conscience, Martin John hits Euston station. Rabbits go home to their warrens. Bus drivers take the bus to the depot. Martin John, in a state, takes his state to Euston. No one is entirely sure why—including Martin John. *It's where I got my head screwed on about what was going on with him—do you understand me now?*

That's all he'll say on Euston.

At Euston, opportunities prevail.
Legs, flesh, feet and trains.
Circuits.
Rain can't fall indoors.

All this heading to Euston means Martin John is sleeping less and less.

Walks more. Sleeps less. Walks more and more. More and more walks with a full bladder. More and more full bladder. Less and less sleep. He has started drinking certain types of water. Believes it fills his bladder faster. More and more he likes his bladder stone-full, pressing against the band of his trousers. Sometimes he pushes it to insist upon pain.

Once he carried an empty water bottle inside the band of his trousers. The top of it peeking up like a reminder. He begins travelling this way, several water bottles sticking out of the top of his waistband. People eye them, they look at the bottles. He smiles. He has caught them looking. I have you now, he thinks. He has their gaze away from Baldy Conscience. Sometimes he'll rapidly rip a bottle up and out and towards his mouth, while looking at the looker, who inevitably looks alarmed, then looks away. Once a woman held his gaze. He didn't like that. She forced him to open the bottle and drink from it by looking and continuing to look at him. One of Baldy's team. No doubt.

Passengers left the train. She did not. Two seats either side of her. He moved over with a plan, but she was onto him. He doesn't recall exactly her words but something along the lines of fucking, bursting, pervert. She put an elbow up to his throat and it threw his head back. He scrambled towards the door. Exited at an unintended station. He didn't think women could do that.

Only women on Baldy's team could do that. Baldy's plants were closing in on him.

···➔

Once he has them with the spout of the water bottle above his trousers, he inches another step further. He lowers his zip. Leaves his fly undone.

They see it.

Of course they see it.

He registers the gaze, the eye-corner glance to confirm. I have you now, he thinks.

···➔

Next he removes his underwear before the zip is lowered.

Easy: hide it behind his coat, reveal and let them have it. Give what is wanted.

They have it. They have what it is they want.

Coats can drift. Open. That's what coats are like. That's what women like, open coats and a quick face full of him. He likes it too. He likes what they like.

···➔

Sometimes though if it's raining, it's not enough. He wants more.

⇢

The other thing is at him again. The thing his mother won't say aloud. So he's not saying it aloud either. The thing she says he has stopped.

He's doing it again.

⇢

Now it's feet. He's started pulling slip-tricks with his foot and their foot, your foot, woman-foot and women-feet and sometimes even woman-legs. Legs are daring. Legs are especially daring on the Underground. Mam told him *I don't want you on the Underground, don't go on the Underground.* She wants him overground where he supposes she can see him. *People make things up on the Underground,* she told him cryptically.

Martin John is back on the Underground. It cannot end well.

⇢

He wants to go between their legs.
He wants to post a letter there.
A letter P, not a B.

⇢

There are certain types of footwear it proves easier with. Boots. Flip-flops and sandals he does not like. He likes that they show flesh, they prove there is a foot, but you cannot allow your foot, or his foot, to drape against a foot or leg without acknowledging it. It will hurt. It will hurt if you wear solid work boots like Martin John wears. All year. All weather. Same type of boot. It's the lower leg he is after; he wants his calf against her calf, whoever she is. Or knee to her flesh. Doesn't matter who she is. Doesn't matter who you are, love. You're incidental. You need only be on the Tube when Martin John's on the Tube, if he decides it's the day to cadge a rub. His leg against a woman's leg. You need only be a woman with a leg. You aren't special, you aren't chosen, you are a woman with a leg. That's it. A leg he finds access to. A leg that happens to be available. That's all you are.

If he doesn't manage it on the Tube, he will attempt likewise on a bench. Sit down beside a woman, fumble with his bags as distraction—Tesco carrier bags with readymade meals work best, they topple perfectly—and drape his leg out so that, for a bitter fraction of a second, before she registers it, his leg will touch hers. Whoever she is. That's it, that's all he wants. Just to smear along her. A light buttering. A smudge. Or at least that's where it starts. Then inevitably he becomes greedy.

If he gets away with small contact he begins to want more. He wishes for summer and shorts and bare flesh. He begins to want to put the palm of his hand on her flesh, whoever she is. (He wants to push his hips up against her.) Ultimately he wants his hand between her legs like a letter.

Often he is curtailed. A head-swiping set of eyes. Her leg will immediately remove from his. Sometimes her whole body will up and depart. Once she was sitting beside her boyfriend. That did not go well. He never ever puts his foot or leg there if a woman is beside a man. Unless the man is old or young, so young he is her child. If she is travelling with a child, he is even more likely to sit down beside her and try it.

Two factors: avoiding Baldy Conscience and if she's with a child. Those are the two distinct, determining factors.

⇢

That time when the British Transport Police cautioned him, how they waited for him on the platform and snuck him away. That was sneaky. That time when they cautioned him he told them he wasn't long back from Beirut. They seemed to buy it. They asked what he'd been doing in Beirut. Things are different here, they said blankly. In Beirut I put my foot on the bus beside a woman's foot and she made no fuss about it. We've had reports about you, they said. You aren't to be lurking around the stations. If we catch you we'll arrest you.

Again, he persisted that he wasn't long back from Beirut. I was fighting in a war there, he said. I went over for my brother's wedding and I was dragged into battle. He didn't like the word arrest. I am like you. I am a military man he wanted the officers to know. You and I, we have been in battle. I am in battle and you too are in battle. We are embattled. They repeated the warning about arrest. They lied and said there had been four complaints about him.

That time when the British Transport Police cautioned him it was the most scared he'd been. If he could not go to Euston it would be very serious. Euston was where he figured many things out. But they couldn't stop him going there. I'm only going to catch a train, he would tell them.

He started buying train tickets. He had to buy train tickets. He was not allowed to stand in the station without a ticket they said. They were after him. Ever after him. They had caught him. Cautioned him. He had been primed.

It meant he had to ride on trains to places he'd rather not be, but he couldn't give up on Euston. He bought a rail card to make the tickets cheaper. He noticed they were chronically looking out for him and he contemplated wearing disguises. I only want to walk around a train station, he reasoned. I only want to walk around Euston Station to be away from Baldy Conscience.

⋯→

Without Euston Station he couldn't do his circuits.
Nor his crosswords.
He had his rituals.
He knew what he needed.
Pork and pies.
Crosswords and circuits were what he needed.
Euston provided all that he needed.

⋯→

He concluded Baldy Conscience was directly behind it. He probably had friends in the force. He paid attention to their accents to see whether they sounded like Baldy Conscience. If they did then they were probably related to Baldy Conscience. They all sounded different. Every one that stopped him had a different accent.

Each time they requested his ticket, which was every time they spotted him at Euston, he told them a little more about his time in Beirut. If they were taking his ticket near the train, he would take up their time. He enacted serious efforts to ensure that he took up their time in the hope it might cull their desire to keep approaching him.

It didn't.

And then it did. It began to keep them away once he talked about the houses and the bread in Beirut. Then he added pigeons and dogs. No one wanted to talk about pigeons nor bread nor moving house. He had the perfect cocktail.

He could cause very long queues with such talk as he pretended to hunt for a ticket that didn't exist. Trains were delayed. Passengers pushed past. People said mate. They waved tickets at the ticket person and careened by. Still he talked. He was inexhaustible on Beirut. He even surprised himself how much the place was providing in the way of queue-forming conversation.

···→

Then he changed the conversation. Near to Christmas he changed the conversation. He talked instead of a suicidal brother whenever they asked him for his ticket. He would talk about his suicidal brother and being on the way to visit him and if they held him here his brother would jump. The passengers behind forced to listen would not push through so fast, nor say mate. They were hungry to hear this story. A story of a man about to jump. Until finally they said things like it was really cruel not to let him on the train. They threatened to buy him a ticket if he wasn't let on since obviously he had a ticket.

The women, it was the women who always stuck up for him, said it was cruel. In a way this puzzled him, until it did not puzzle him—like all of it he grew used to it. He became what it needed him to become in order to enact what he felt he must enact.

--->

The next time he saw that particular guard he told him
—He died you know. He died that day. He died waiting on
me. He jumped from the top of a car park in Birmingham.
It did not ever occur to Martin John that no train went to
Birmingham from Euston.

—Sorry mate. Sorry to hear that. Have you got your ticket?

For that conversation, without fail, he would have a
ticket. He'd buy the cheapest ticket on whatever route.
Ride the train. Step off next station and turn right back
around on the next train.

They forgot to look for him exiting the train.

He could manage a few circuits when they were not looking for him. That was how it was if he was to manage to
do the circuits.

The circuits are the only thing keeping me sane, he'd
exhale as he swerved into the corners of the station. Rain
will fall, rain will fall—he spoke aloud to diffuse his anger.

--->

Once he took the suicidal-brother story so far that he
crumpled down on the floor in front of the ticket man
and started heaving. He cried hard. So hard he had no
idea what he was crying about. When they, the public,
asked him what was wrong, he shrugged and stood up.
He knows what's wrong, he said, indicating the perplexed
ticket collector as he began to leave the station.

--->

If he found a girlfriend who worked at the station and who
would vouch for him, then they might never be able to ban

him from Euston entirely. He likes Mary who works at the bakery, whom he talks to about God and the Bible.

It was a thought he had once. It passed. He remembered the warnings. The many, many warnings. He recalled why it was not a good idea. She would probably be a plant sent by Baldy Conscience. She would probably torment him. She would never ultimately agree to be his girlfriend. She might pretend she was interested and that would be it. Until she'd laugh. There would be a moment where she'd laugh at him. To his face. He'd created alternative moments. Fearful ones. He liked women afraid of him. If they were afraid of him, they were his. If they were afraid of him Baldy Conscience could not prevail. He would only send the kind ones after Martin John, for they'd be bound up in his convoluted and exceptional plan to sink him. The way they had all been, all the way along, from the moment he stepped off that ferry, going as far back as his mother. He firmly believed that Baldy Conscience must have been sourced and solicited by mam. She could call him off. At any point she could say *surrender and call him off.* Why didn't she do that?

...→

He phoned mam for the first time outside Euston.

—Call him off, he said. Call him off.

—Call who off?

—Him upstairs.

—If I have told you once I have told you a million times, what did I tell you—stop going upstairs.

—Call him off. Tell him to stop.

—Tell who to stop? What are you saying? And while we are at it, she added, enough with the parcels. Stop sending that filth. It's disgusting.

—Call him off, he repeated, or Rain will fall.

—You're telling me, she said. Well that's the one thing I can guarantee: there's never no shortage on rain.

153

→

After that, he knew they were in cahoots. The way they both made light of the weather. One day early on when Martin John warned him of approaching rain and the need for a hat, Baldy Conscience had laughed at him. Umbrella Man was likely also sent by the two of them. Who'd bring an umbrella to the toilet? Who would do that? Only somebody wearing an umbrella as a uniform. A uniform that had a story attached.

They had lost him his job.

What was the final chapter so? Would it end at Euston?

---→

Mam has been receiving strange brown packets containing a travel brochure with pornographic pictures taped inside them. The pictures are folded into small squares. To properly see them there are flaps she must unpeel first. Even though she knows what they contain she opens every one of them for proof. It's the signal.

They can only be coming from one person. The next time he phones, she'll let him have it.

He does not phone.

She waits.

He does not phone.

Another brown envelope lands.

She waits.

He does not phone.

The time has come.

To go over.

And bring him back.

It's finished.

---→

There's also the letter in her hall.

From the solicitor.

From the girl.

He can come back and face it.

The pictures confirm the letter.
Her doubt has evaporated.
There's only one way to deal with such fellas.
The people in the *Daily Mail* are right.

⋯➔

HE IS CONVINCED THAT BALDY CONSCIENCE WANTS TO SHOOT HIM, PROBABLY AT EUSTON STATION. HE HAS NOTICED ALL THE STORIES IN THE NEWSPAPERS OF HARM DONE. HARM WAS DONE. THERE ARE REASONS ENOUGH HARM IS DONE. BALDY CONSCIENCE HAS FOUND THE REASON TO HARM HIM. HE HAS FOUND OUT THAT HARM WAS DONE.

WHAT THEY DON'T KNOW:

Of what Martin John is convinced.

Martin John has decided that wherever Baldy Conscience lives, beside whomever, however he lives, he will, inevitably, put someone in a hospital. Therefore he is committed to suffering him until Baldy Conscience is defeated. It is rabidly unfair that one man can inflict so much misery on an unknowing population. Martin John has come to know this. He knows about these things. He is ahead in this loop. The rest of us are behind him. He has the knowledge. He won't say it aloud but this is a vision. He is a visionary in regard to Baldy Conscience. Therefore it's up to him to deal with the BC.

Baldy Conscience has arrived at him in order to be dealt with. Baldy Conscience was sent. Baldy Conscience is now doing the sending. Martin John is the post office in this transaction. He, Martin John, is being transacted through. Evil going in, evil going out, evil going in-between his organs. He will be made an example of one way or the other. He has been made an example of. He conveniently forgets what brought him to this city. He conveniently forgets they are watching out for him at Euston. All these incidentals are spliced inside the Baldy gallop which consumes him. All appetites that govern him are likely controlled by Baldy Conscience. How many more are being controlled? Everywhere he turns he can see elements of Baldy Conscience's control. The man is legendary in his ability to spread distrust, despair and detritus. On the streets, the buses, the television, the damage that Baldy Conscience is doing becomes apparent.

He, Martin John, will do what the world has requested of him. He will do what 'til now every man and woman has shirked from. It will be unpleasant and it will smell, but it must be done before this man undoes one and all.

He will make it impossible for Baldy to stay. He will sabotage the plumbing, the sink, the sewer, whatever it takes. Back it up, up there, and that will send Baldy tumbling down and out.

⋯→

He takes a spanner, some carrier bags, and a big onion up the stairs, bolts himself into the bathroom and thinks. The bathroom, a limited rectangle with the basic apparatus included, has suffered in his absence. Baldy Conscience has created a volcano of a towel and sock pile. He's draped his dirty clothes, spent plastic razors, empty deodorant bottles, sweet foils, crisp wrappers, cigarette cartons and newspapers all over the floor. There is no sign of toilet paper, which registers immediate alarm for Martin John. How is the man wiping his arse? This may not be his business, nor does he wish it to become his concern—he is aware of the dangers if he ponders it too long—but he lifts up the newspaper from the bathroom floor to discover Badly Conscience has been using his archive of Eurovision newspapers in the place of the common man's approach to bathrooming himself, the sane person's employment of a fucking toilet roll. The stuff manufactured for the task.

Carefully, slowly, he retrieves what remains of this paper, examines the date and tries to calculate how many years' worth of his treasure Baldy has been balling, searing, tearing up to wipe himself. It's devastating to discover the depth this uncultured zombie will sink too. Tonight, tomorrow, any night that has not yet approached, the battle is on. If he cannot force Baldy Conscience to exit, he will bar him outside. He will replace the exit push with an entry bar. This will mean he, Martin John, will have to remain inside the house, until he, Baldy Conscience, pushes off or gives up all hope of ever gaining entry again.

Like all his plans, Martin John must execute this one with careful attention. If he wants Baldy Conscience out and permanently out, Martin John must ready up to remain permanently in. The man who refuses to budge will prevail. If he has learnt nothing from Baldy Conscience he has learnt that.

⋯→

> **Inadequate:** The inadequate molester is the sex offender who least resembles social and behavioural norms. He is characterized as a social misfit, an isolate, who appears unusual or eccentric. He may be mentally ill and prefers non-threatening sexual partners.

⋯→

WHAT THEY KNOW:

Before.

Once mam was more direct with Martin John:
I am glad it is finished she wrote.
I am glad you have stopped.
I am glad you are done with it.

←···

They beat him. They beat him hard and relentless. Then
they beat him again. It was because of the incident outside
SuperValu they beat him. That's what he thought. But it
could have been another incident. The incidents backed
up, formed a retroactive queue. He longed to know which
incident had sent them because a response, whatever form
it took, was victory. He derived pleasure from their aggres-
sion. They desired him. He noticed this. He liked the
desire. That they desired to pummel him, secondary to the
reasons they felt they needed to.

···→

There was a baring incident outside the SuperValu
Supermarket in the small town. She was the one that took
him out. Or was it the other one, the later one? He longed
to know, to have a chart, a recording, to indicate which girl
or young woman had knocked him off the island precisely.

He had kept going and going. He had made it seem to
mam that he'd stopped, but all the while he was still at it
in slow and pin-sticking ways. Small rubs here, a nudge
there, a hand over the line, all leading up, leading on, leading under the band. He wants under the band of skirts
and trousers. Hand down. Hand up. He was watching. He
waited. Sometimes he moved.

It was rough calculating who might let out a yell or raise
hell or ream him yonder. He was random. Mostly random.
But there was one girl he went back at a few times. She

was the only one who ever really seemed scared. Martin John would say he went back as contrition to let her know he wasn't so bad and hadn't meant it that way, the way it seemed. But instead he found himself back with abandon, trying harder to go further, trying always to re-raise that first alarm he elicited from her. Those eyes. She had no brothers he was sure. He did the worst stuff to her and no brother ever came after him. Was this why he went back? He couldn't tell you. It doesn't do for Martin John to get too active in the thinking around all this. It is rooted in defiance. In the back of his head, he has his mother's face primed. Each and every time he makes such a move—and there have been more incidences than his fingers and toes could count thrice—he is catapulted by his mother's gaze. It is the band that fires him. Or that is what he'd have us believe. But we're not fooled. We're onto you Martin John, more than you may realize.

⋯➔

Maybe 12 years of age this one, the age where early bumps of flesh are filling out, and he, the elder, can imagine small mounds of her in his mouth. Inside the shop he had breezily followed her about, noted her selection of chicken breasts and rashers. When she stopped at the fridge and examined packs of sausages, he watched her turn the packet over with her fingers and squish-/squeeze-/squelch-/press-even the tips of them. She peered in at them.

She lifted the packet to her nose and, strangely, smelt it. Absentish, she could be holding anything. Maybe she was thinking of a boy, he prospected, or a pop song or a hairdryer. Clairol, wasn't that the name of a hair dryer? He exited the shop ahead of her to anticipate her route home.

He recalled a group of four girls at this checkout years earlier. He was nearby and observed them behave fidgety around a boy queuing to pay for a packet of crisps. They failed to notice him, but he did not fail to notice they noticed the other lad. He recorded something of that, kept the rind of it as a reminder. The other boy was indifferent to the girls' attention; he was reading an offer on the back of the crisp packet. An older woman walked past and asked that boy something, likely about his mother. He was responsive, warm. Martin John watched as the girls vied for the boy's attention by stealing a glance at him and then speaking just a little bit louder and shaking their hair over their shoulders, sticking one hip out and adjusting their clothes. He was, at that time, older than the boy. He was aware that none had ever performed thus for him.

⋯➔

It was a risk to allow that she might walk down this alley. A lotto-notion that she could cut through here. He was going to try to talk to her. Maybe tease her about smelling the sausages. He had not planned to take it out. But as she approached and noticed him there, she looked away. He didn't like that. He didn't like that she wasn't looking at him. She wasn't looking at him the way he'd seen other girls stare and rummage around that boy with the crisps. Yet she chose this route. She chose this route because she knew he'd be there. She didn't choose another route. That might have lifted him. If she had obviously avoided him. Ha! That would be progress then. It wasn't enough. He would have her attention. He would have her attention no matter what it took. No matter if he only had it for five seconds, he would have it and he knew just how to get it.

⋯→

How'd he navigate the zip so fast?

⋯→

He'd prepared. His hand was in his underwear. Wrapped around it. Had she or had she not looked away? He wouldn't have known. He couldn't have known. Had he imagined she'd look away?

It didn't matter as she was nearer to him now. If he turned his back and swerved around at this dead-on angle she could not escape seeing what he would present to her. It was fast, fleshy-fast. He pulled it up and down a few times as a commencement speech. A mere throat-clearing before the pounce of pronouncement. He wanted an obvious moment in her eyes where she registered it. It would need to be out. It would need to be hard. Hard. Out. Pointed at her. (Not out, down and limp.) Her feet making that putt-surr sound on the ground had it hardening. Her hand rustling the carrier bag. She was doing all the work for him. Good girl, he thought. That made it stiffen even more. Good girl, he thought again. Come, come on, come on, come on now. Stood sidewards against the wall of a house then rotated a rapid squint over his shoulder to time the turn to her passing. She was closer than he'd calculated. He swung on her, lifted his chin and worked his two hands more forcefully below. One to pull aside his jean fabric, the other to hoik it up and over further, protrude it at her. Direct, flat-eyed, he pulled. He pulled defiant, he pulled transported. Pulled and pulled and pulled. Plumpendicular, he slapped it against his other hand. It was a mere three seconds until he nailed her gaze. Nailed it to his groin.

⋯➔

Except it didn't quite work. It did not work. She barely gave 2 seconds of notice to the site. Calm, elevated, she plodded past with her fist clenched onto the carrier-bag handle. It was not as it had been with other girls: she didn't allow registration. He had taken it out and gone to a lot of trouble. It was a lot of trouble to take it out, he thought, dejected. She had not responded. Something was wrong. They always responded. That was the point in taking it out. It was guaranteed, where words could fail you. It could infiltrate the most desultory, absent gaze. Where words might fail him, the sight of his pound of flesh could penetrate.

⋯➔

After it he didn't feel bad as much as flat. Flatness was what he felt. Like he'd lost interest in something. It was done now. There was a time early on when he'd felt guilty. Now he defaulted to again, again. He would go back for her.

⋯➔

That was the moment it did not work, it did not work the way it previously worked and it was the moment he could have predicted they would come for him.

⋯→

They beat him. Beat him hard. Elbows to his stomach, knee to the groin and into his drooping, saggy pouches. They did not spare his eyes. There was no space for explanation, which was useful because he had no explanation to offer. The bridge of his nose was imprinted with the clasp of a watch. The top of his head was cut. His eye. They marked him in a way he could not leave the house.

What did you say, what did you say? Did you call for help? mam would later ask him.

—I said nothing. I said nothing. I had nothing to say.

He said it flat. Dull, ambivalent like the entire episode took place in his sleep.

—I expected it, he added.

She did not like that. But neither did she ask why. These days she never suggested calling the Guards. They've little time for the likes of us, she said. Unless it is we they are after.

⋯→

With a similar careful attention and calculation, that girl's brothers arrived for him. Two, this one sent. Double the force, double the words, double the sting. Yet only one explanation. The same explanation. The one explanation Martin John refuses to give. He allows mam her own explanation.

—We've to get you out, mam said when she saw the state of him. If you can't stop it, we've to stop it.

Could he stop it? What would he stop?

—Stop what, he said. She will not go further. She would never give voice to that which she wished stopped.

169

⇢

With a similar careful attention and calculation, mam plans for him. With a similar careful attention mam detains him. She keeps him indoors. She kept him indoors. She organized around the damage, his damage. She did dress his wounds. Resentfully.

Whatever you did to deserve this. . . she muttered. She could hardly leave him bleeding at her table. They moved forward. She had questions she chose not to ask. We've to get you out, she said as she pat, pat, patted around the scrapes and incisions. Cuts from fists and knuckles. Punched-in digs and fisty bruises.

I'll kill you, one brother told him as a fist smacked his jaw. Another had his eyes up against his face, so close he could see the man's dirt-packed skin pores. Bruises, knuckle and ring, fist tracks formed mounds around his eyes, his jaw and the side of his head. Every strike had layered itself onto him.

Harm was done.

WHAT MAM KNEW.

There might be further abrasions before she could get him out.

There were rumours. Gossip she refused to believe. Slander she scuffed off. People talk, refuted. There were rumours about Martin John that reached her, the way there were rumours about that man in Galway that reached her and that other fella in Kilkenny who ran to Amsterdam. It was in the papers. People would affirm, Oh him. Sure people knew exactly what he was at, he'd been doing it for years, or, It was only a matter of time.

Evil. Pure evil. Pure deviant sick evil. Adjectives combusted beside reason: there were people who did these things, that she did not dispute. But she could barely get her son to take his socks off all these years, so the public-exposure rumours were ridiculous and malicious. He sometimes kept his hat on indoors. He might be a bit of an odd shilling, but not that odd.

Who had seen it?

Show me the videotape, she planned to ask. Show me the videotape and he's yours. He's yours with a ribbon on him. There are enough cameras about the place these days, if he was doing what was implied, he'd be captured.

There was hearsay that reached her as warnings. Or illumination. They were pressed gently enough to her ear. People customized it as questions, they sought her opinion on news stories. What did she know about this or that and could these perverts be healed? They wanted her speculation. I can only deal with the facts. She disappointed them. In my eyes, a man or woman is only guilty a minute after the jury says so. Until that day, in my eyes, he or she is innocent. She was inclusive. She never let a she alone. If women wanted equality, they could all be equally at fault.

There had been rumours for a while.

Rumours were delivered as questions in these parts.

What could a woman like her do about rumours like those?

Girl rumours were worse. Because he was a boy she didn't pay much heed.

She believed boys were rumoured about for no reason. The girls with the protruding tummies no longer wanted to face their actions and were turning on the boys. All of them. If you let them at you, she would say, what can you expect? When we had chastity in this country we hadn't any such problems.

That was the roundabout exit she chose.

He did it. He did not do it. He could have done it. She made it up. Except there was more than one *she* now.

Rumours and warnings were not evidence.

She worried how it would affect his sisters.
If he had sisters.
She worried if it got out or they came home how could they be married in the church. She worried about the sisters he didn't have.
She worried if it got out how could they prove he hadn't done it?
She worried he had done it. She began to believe he had.
She had seen enough to confirm it.

It was when he did it to a man she really panicked.
She really, really panicked.
If he was taking it out and waving it at a man, it meant it was highly likely he wouldn't have spared a woman.
Then she got a straight head on her.
Then she got him out.
To London.

⇢

But not before he got at the girl waiting in the dentist's office.

⇢

If he ever came back they'd kill him.
It was simple. He could not come back.
He had complicated it.
As if it were not complicated enough already.
This list is inside the teapot with the other lists.
She did all her reckoning on the back of receipts.
Her writing had to become smaller and smaller to fit the explanations on the back of the receipts.
When it was all said and done there was an inventory in this teapot.
It sat as evidence.
If there was a fire, it would all be destroyed.
Then she remembered the teapot would not catch fire.
It would be retained.
What would you do?
This would be the final receipt she would write on and place back in the teapot.
What would you do?
The next time he was admitted to hospital, she would bring the teapot and turn its contents onto the table and let the doctor see it all.
See the mistakes I made, she would tell him.

She went to confession.
She didn't mention the mistakes.
She did tell the priest that she was writing things on the back of papers and storing them in teapots.
He asked, Were they bad things? She said they were.

It had happened before. Mam knows this. Yet she'll try to squeeze this information to the back of her eyes or to the left of the situation. My memory is going, she'll say. It's the stress, she'll say. It's very difficult, she'll say.

Yet she knows the first moment she thought Martin John might be taking strange. He was stood in the hall in front of a religious picture she still has there on the wall with his trousers down. Except he was stood with the religious picture removed from the wall and placed on a chair. He was stood there with his hands inside his underpants. She passed him in a whoosh and retrieved the Mother of God's picture, pressed it into her cardigan, moved promptly to stand up on a kitchen chair and hang the woman back up.

It was the way he did not rush to cover himself up. It was his non-reaction that frightened her. She had to go back and call his name and tell him *get dressed. Stop standing there, someone might come to the door.* She should have said, Have you lost your mind? Instead she allowed her concern to remain with who else might see him rather than what he was doing.

She had ignored it, or fudged it. Whatever she had not done, she's paying for.

⋯→

The disassociation was only the start. He became more flagrant. He'd lie in his bed with his bum bare to the ceiling, head down, and wait 'til she came in to find him. She could call and call and call him to the kitchen for his tea and he wouldn't budge. She'd go down to the room, find him in that state and he'd issue a peal of laughter when she came in.

—What's that? he'd say, lifting his head.
—I'm calling you.
—I can hear that, he'd say.

—What are you doing?

—I am waiting to be heard.

—What are you doing? Why aren't you dressed?

What would follow was difficult. He'd rise and saunter past her, letting his parts drift and wobble. He'd have swiped her with them were they long enough to do so. The way in which he'd look at her was odd. Calculated and vicious. Deviant, she thought in retrospect.

⋯➔

See how still no one mentions the girl?

⋯➔

He would leave the bathroom door unlocked. He would want her to walk in on him. Whether he was bathing or not. Once she found him sat on top of the toilet-seat cover yanking at his parts. When she stuttered an apology: *God, sorry*, and *lock the door*, he stared her in the eye and pulled even harder at the exposure below. Like it didn't matter whether she was there or not. He'd carry on.

She never entered any door, any place, without knocking. Even when she pushed the door in, she automatically protected herself now by closing her eyes. She did this as she approached any door that was closed, even if she went to the doctor's. She never assumed what she would find behind a door would be a normal, clothed human being, behaving in a normal, clothed manner.

⋯➔

Still no word on the girl. Or that mam knows that he did what the girl said he did.

⟶

It became sinister and more sinister. She became afraid of him.

We have to get you out, became an unuttered *be gone because I am afraid of you*. You and your possibilities exhaust me. I will be relieved to hand you off so someone else may worry about you.

⟶

He knows this today as an adult and has considered admitting it, except no opportunity has come up. Harm was done said aloud is as far as he'll go until you ask him to go further. Who will ask him? Will you ask him? Should I ask him? Who asks these people? Are they ever asked outside a courtroom or must we get them into a courtroom to pose the question: Just what the fuck do you think you were doing or thinking? Tell us this at your leisure. We are gathered here to hear you. Finally.

He will admit that he did not back off. Not that day in the dentist's waiting room. There is a moment when you back off, when you make the decision not to proceed, when your brain acknowledges the signal, but on he ploughed. He could tell you he ploughed on because he wanted to, but usually he'll only tell you what he has told her: I don't know. I don't know. I don't remember.

⟶

He couldn't tell mam he does remember.
Harm was done is all he could tell her.
Harm was done by him.

But she will want details and he doesn't have details. He's cobwebbed them in behind the blankness of Harm was done.

Once, in a dim moment, they forced him to remember. He slipped up. Or one doctor slipped him up. She was a student and he can't remember how she asked the question but it was in some kind of assessment. But he slipped and admitted. They drugged it out of him.

They drugged him when they took him in. Said if he didn't calm down they'd have to give him something to calm him down. He told them nine different ways in nine different languages that no way was he calming down. He held onto the newspaper he'd attacked the man in the shop for. The man who called him a savage. Or the other man beside him. All of it. Baldy back at home watching telly, ruining his life's work. She talked him into the topic and out of the topic and around the topic and then they had talked about it, but by the end he remembered how to deny it and it came back to him and he denied everything he'd said even though it was only minutes since he said it. He was surprised she did not look more wounded. She was blank about it. This troubled him. It troubled him that she didn't demand more. If she railed on him, he could back off, but the way she sat there still as jam and gave nothing away was trickier. At the end of the session, she reminded him the session was taped. He left furious. Furious that she caught him, furious that he couldn't just forget. Then within a few hours he couldn't quite recall why he was furious.

If they're going to keep taping me it'll be very hard to admit to things, he reasoned.

And he commenced with 'but,' 'and another thing,' to confound and make himself indecipherable.

⋯→

Anytime any person remotely connected to the mental services came near him he commenced and ended his sentences these two ways. This he enforced as the means not to tell them anything further, not to be confessing to things he could not recall, nor even recall confessing to, once he'd confessed. He told mam about what he was doing. I am only talking to them two ways, he said.

—Good, she said, if I have told you once I have told you a thousand times to stop talking and shut up. For the love of God shut up.

—And another thing, he said.

—Shut up.

—But . . .

—Shut up.

He had it right. His testing process had succeeded.

⟶

It was an awful lot of work, but he had to teach Baldy Conscience a transdermal lesson. Other people rigged with better fists would have merely punched Baldy Conscience or kicked him in the arse down the stairs and out the front door. He had not that constitution. He had the hanging-around-the-post-box and waiting-on-a-shift constitution. He had the walking in circles and avoiding-the-gaze-of-those-who-were-clearly-out-to-get-him look, from the top of the academy to the men in manholes, all of whom were conspiring, he didn't doubt, from the elbow-directing of Mr Baldy Conscience. To take him out would require taking out the whole planet, something he found 7 days in the week wasn't enough to achieve. What could he control? He could control the language that wiped this man's arse. Once he'd recovered from the shock and awfulness of finding his treasured Eurovision archive heading up the man's bum, he replaced those precious papers with every depraved story published. Since there was a non-stop supply of them, he'd merely to collate and create a pile of papers that included them. Baldy Conscience was blithely tearing strips off the paper during his daily trips to the seat. He was going to blast the plumbing, this was clear, but that was a problem he'd accept for the newfound control he had.

The other problem was Martin John was going back upstairs again.
 Back upstairs meant he was using the toilet again.
 Back upstairs meant new danger.
 She'd warned him.
 And another thing,
 Shut up, she'd said.

WHAT THEY DON'T KNOW:

The girl.

SHE
Remembers
How
he crawled across the carpet on his knees, like a strange creepy cat, and coiled his cold hand firmly round the top part of her leg, way up under her skirt. This is the motion she remembers.

That is why it was not a mistake. He did not hesitate. He said he didn't remember.

Nobody saw.

When she told them they shook their heads and asked, was she sure?

She was sure until they asked.

⋯➔

Get off! She said.

He did not get off. He held on harder. Tighter. He had her by the leg. She was his.

⋯➔

More questions.

Until it was reduced to, So he only put his cold hand on your leg you are saying?

We've to be very careful accusing people in these situations.

Situations where nobody sees are complicated.

Witnesses, you need witnesses.

A report like this could ruin a person's life.

Unless someone saw.

I saw.

He saw.

He says he doesn't remember.

And she became confused about what was and was not meant to be. Until it was all reduced to, if he didn't do anything other than put his hand on you was there any harm done?

Harm was done.

Harm was done and further harm would be done.

····→

Get off, she repeated. She shook her encased leg hard. She kicked at him.

He did not get off.

He moved in with his other hand. Balled up into a fist. Punched her. Right there. In the vagina. Thunk.

Pain. Sharp pain.

Again. Harder. Stronger. He pounded. That balled-up right fist.

Smack. A hard hit to her pubic bone. It was as though he'd ironed that fist to achieve the perfect flat shape, to achieve the perfect hit.

He didn't speak a word.

It hurt.

Soar.

Sore.

She roared.

The reception woman came around to see.

The reception woman definitely saw his fist up by her skirt because she shouted at him to stop it, let her go. Leave her alone.

The phone rang, which dragged her back to the window.

····→

....→

Did she, the girl, remember?

Because he didn't remember and remember, if he didn't remember, then how could they ascertain who did remember? And who would be more likely to remember? There was a thesaurus of vagueness about remembering. Between all the remembering she grew anxious, weary and retreated. Maybe she didn't remember either? It was easier not to remember.

But now she remembers.

His mother's visit.

The threats.

The hinted threat.

The hint beneath the threat.

The hinterland of threat.

That intra-land of threat.

How she has lived in it.

....→

Today, a 32-year-old mum with two kids, she was still living in it. She was living in it as she put the washing on the line. As she picked up the phone at work. Once when she sent a text, it came to her. Who was this guy anyway? Who was this guy to be putting his hand on her leg? What the fuck was his hand doing there? 20 years later, as she is sending a text, she is still asking questions that may not be answered.

Whenever she is nervous for her children, she remembers.

She remembers when she is nervous for her children. Never lets them alone. Calculates each and every situation for potential. The presentation of a smidgen of opportunity never evades her. She sees it widescreen, close up, speculative and resolute. It's never just a dismissed or shrugged-off possibility; it is an imminent, immediate probability.

She never lets her children sleep the night at any house, apartment, bunk bed but hers. This is how she remembers. It is within those decisions she remembers. Every person she comes into contact with she must assess for danger. This is how she remembers it. Within the cracks of possibility she remembers.

Her husband she chose for his gentleness. He does not inspire passion in her. But he is safe. Non-paroxysmal. (His name Mick.) He is exactly what her granny told her to look for in a partner. A nice man, she said. Find a nice, decent fella. No drink or drama, granny said.

She does not remember whether granny said that before or after the thing happened. She does not remember whether granny too asked if she remembered. She only remembers granny said nice, decent. Her husband never puts his hand on her 'til she invites him to. That's why she chose him.

⋯➔

The pain revisits her like a phantom limb. Never quite gone.

Sound too.

She remembers that sound years beyond, high up under her skirt. The smacking thunk.

The way bone reverberates if you hit it with direct force. How pain shoos along it. And the way his other hand tightened around her right leg in victory.

185

It was in restraint he achieved his victory. It was his eyes. He wanted to be there and he wanted to do what he was doing, that was what she read in them. A sadistic spark. If eyes could laugh those eyes were smirking.

She still did not understand how he landed the punch. So specific, even though she had thrashed his force off. The precision—was that the worst? Or being pinned?

It came down to who remembered and when they remembered. He maintained he didn't recall and then he began to recall and add perplexing details into the mix to throw them off the trail.

⋯→

The girl, which one? There had been a few. A few complained. A few he was surprised *didn't* complain, a few he knew would never complain. He became more adept at figuring out which girl belonged to which group. He became more adept at getting closer to them through anonymous means. You could bump up against them on the bus. You could rest your hand on places accidentally. Feet were good this way. He could move them close. Very close 'til they nearly touched. Then tap the stranger's foot or leg and retract suddenly. It gave him a spritz. A buzz. It was a bite.

⋯→

The woman saw. The woman from the reception saw. She came around. She saw him with his hand on her leg.

Stop that messing! She said. Before I have to call the dentist out to deal with you two. Did she think them siblings?

She blurted. He hurt me, he hurt me, he hurt me. Hiccupy pleading. Stop now, she said again.

The woman behind the reception—a nice woman who chatted to her mother and every mother and could even

186

be seen at the shops, at church, at a school sports day—brought her behind the desk and gave her sweets from her bag and told that young fella, him, to sit in the chair and if he moved again his mother would hear about it. The nice woman who chatted to mothers did not ask what he had done because the phone rang. She did brush the hair out of the girl's eyes. She did call out an instruction to the dentist on an unrelated matter.

⋯➔

He had had to thump her through her skirt. He did not manage to get a direct hit. Even though he'd tried. He fought that fabric and she kicked him with whatever small leg she had available.

⋯➔

This was the small thing she held onto, that her flesh was still hers, because he had only managed to assault her through fabric. Years later, this would be consolation.

But how it stung. The pain hovered underneath/beneath her. Each time she sat on her bicycle it came back. There was no dispute among the bruises that lined her pubic bone about who remembered what. Nor who saw what. It was stamped onto them.

⋯➔

It was a time when people didn't see stuff. That was the time it was.

⤏

When his mother came, the nice woman who could be seen at football, at the shop, at church and always at the dentist, asked how was she getting on. They talked about the weather. The nice woman said he, her son, had grown. He's a grand tall lad, she said. She said nothing about what had happened.

⤏

Mam said if this was only being sprung on her now, so many years later, *it was very suspicious Martin John* and *where something is suspicious, suspicion can be calmed for there's never been a man convicted on suspicion unless he was planting bombs* and Martin John had planted no bombs. She could be sure of that, she said lightly.

Nobody said anything to me when I entered that room. If there were things to be said, they would have been said, but the guards coming round now or rumours of questions going to be asked were not good. They are not good Martin John. They are not good for any of us now, you know that?

And for the forty-fifth time she would ask, as she always did ask, *tell me again what you remember*. It certainly wasn't for the lack of asking.

⋯→

Mam said I can't save you.

She never said the truth. The truth is THEY ARE COMING FOR HIM. How long has she known about Baldy Conscience?

Did she maybe send him? Have they met?

Did they meet at Euston?

Was it mam who told him to go do the circuits at Euston?

No. No. That's not it. She said keep the head down. She said she didn't want him on the Tube. She said *Keep the head down, Into bed at night, Don't mind anybody and they won't be minding you either.* She said other things. He cannot remember the other things. Did she warn him about Baldy Conscience? How did she know about Beirut?

He is confused. Painfully confused. He must walk. He must settle this question of what mam knows.

⋯→

It is in walking that opportunity presents.

He sees her. A her. He sees a tree. It's tempting. He can put his back to the tree. He can swing round at her when she passes. He lets this one go though. She has too sad a walk. Her hair is too long. She might hide her face and that would be a waste. Also he does not know who might be lurking on the Elephant & Castle Road waiting to batter him between his eyes.

He takes *it* instead to King's Cross station.

A nice metal seat. In the Underground he sits on it, solid beneath his trap. Hands in pockets can climb down below and release the sneaky out to be peeked at. It's a gurgle, a gurgling thrill, a r-rr-rrr, as they step off the Tube and he sits there on cold metal, his lower back supported. Moves hands to his two thighs and lets it sit out there, open-air trousers, orbiting just above the seat. It is out. Out and it's all for them. The more people who descend, the more of it he reveals. Leans further back. Lounges. Arms wide behind his head. Them all penetrating him with their eyes. In-between another train, he hoists his balls up and out of his underpants. Leans back, all of it displayed. His tubey swollen. Ha!

He does not close his legs as the transport police approach him. Sits there and stares out at them, like they have imagined the flesh and protrusion he's displaying. Like everyone else, they want him too.

He does not say much when they bring him in for questioning. Even when they ask him to fasten his trousers he is very slow to respond. He says he can't close his trousers and he needs her, the policewoman, to close them for him. Martin John feels out of it and tells them he has no idea where he is or what his name is. They tell him they are aware of what his name is. They warn him. They caution him. Next time he's going to be charged.

···→

He phones mam and tells her that the police have arrested him and he is being cautioned and released and will maybe go to a prison or a clinic.

She tells him to stop talking rubbish and above all to get out to Noanie on Wednesday.

—You aren't capable of getting arrested. They are not interested in you. So get over yourself and stop dreaming, would you.

···→

It is true that he has phoned her a number of times to tell her he is in prison and she is fed up of discovering that he is not in prison.

Once he phoned her from Beirut. That did not go so well because he was at Waterloo Station and she could hear a man at the phone box roaring Fucking hurry up or I'll burst you.

She does not believe him anymore. He would be in a coffin before she'd believe he could be dead.

⋯➔

He likes trees.

Trees could entice.

Trees were good for lolling against.

Where there was lolling it urged his up. Even the sight of tree bark made him nervous, because he could put his back against it and if his back is against something, there's more likelihood he'll take *it* out and swing *it* around on them. Once he lolls it is like sitting into a car seat. Clunk click, on goes the belt. Or, in this case, off comes the belt and down goes the zip. The early fumble, tip, mutter, gave urge to surge, a shout from below at the sight of her, any her, but especially the one he'd selected, with her eyes on him, on *it* specifically. Now. Because the women love it and in those moments lapped up that he'd chosen them and that he'd share it with them. They were mad for it until they realized they were not mad for it and that was when the trouble started. But nothing could take from the early part. The first nub. The introduction if you like. Nub to stub to engorge. Persist tenaciously 'til she looks. She must look. She shall look. She is looking. Big wide smile beside his eyes, up by his head bone. The delight could have expanded his skull.

And then he didn't care what she liked or didn't like. It switched from the pounding of enticement to only his solo delectation at delivery. If violence followed, so be it. He considered violence celebratory now. That, she, whoever she was, would find cause to report on him, that she'd have to repeat something of what she saw and what he did. That she'd need to pass along details sufficient that it would anger a father, a brother, a boyfriend. Spring him to fury. Ultimately then, he'd nabbed two of them. She had to open her mouth and speak of him, even if she would not speak *to* him.

····➔

When things were bad he felt they were coming for him. He felt it every minute of any day when things were bad. He made signs that indicated this and placed them all over the house. Another reason he needed the house empty of tenants. The signs had to be written out and they needed to be hung up or left in corners so they'd catch his eye.

He wrote these instructions often during the bad times. He wrote them in black marker on the back of double LPs. He wrote them on abandoned lumps of hardboard. He wrote them on the covers of his Eurovision videos. He listed what needed to happen for him to be good. He placed one such sign in the front window of his house. Once he ran out of things to make signs on he would settle and watch the same videotape over and over. In between he would pace to the front window, and if he wasn't satisfied, would open the front door, step out and read the sign aloud. Sometimes he left the front door open after he did that, like someone passing might come in and agree with him. They'd settle down and he'd be guarded.

⋯➔

When things are not good, mam was right, he had made them this way. It's a mess entirely of your own creation, she'd say. He tried to keep writing instructions, but at number 4 often became confused and lost his way. He wrote instructions that were not relevant. No smoking, no drinking, no smoking, no drinking, no fizzy drinks. Then the instructions puzzled him. He felt pursued and would lift the phone and begin making calls.

⋯➔

Martin John is amazed at how thoughts of Baldy Conscience can provoke him to a dark and low place. He's darkly amazed, sinister amazed, razed amazed. Take today. Martin John has not been able to move. That man and all he symbolizes have him stewed. Stuck to the edge of his barmy-looking bed surrounded by his towers of videotapes and Eurovision memorabilia like a battlement. He sits. He seethes. Sometimes in the night the piles topple in on him. He has a reflex for removing them. He can gently push them off with a foot if need be. They incur no damage.

Last night, and late last night at that, and maybe even this morning, when he should have been sleeping, he was roused instead by the gargle above. The howlin' and hootin' of that man still going long after the moon himself had gone to bed. Baldy Conscience has been going all night. He's up there. There are guitars up there. There might even be a brass band up there. There's men up there and Martin John doesn't like it. He doesn't like it because where there's men, sometimes there's a woman even.

Among the violent possibilities that occur to Martin John as to how he should deal with Baldy Conscience, the possibility of slamming a tambourine down on his head and allowing that bullocky dome to split the skin until it sinks, tinkling round his neck. The tinkling would settle a humiliation upon Baldy Conscience that another man might not notice. Martin John had noticed him big on sounds: the cunt word on the telephone, the carping sounds in the bathroom, the sniffing and strange caulking sounds in the back of his throat. Baldy Conscience was always on the brink of a sniff. There was never a sniff far from him and yet he exhibited tremendous control. Martin John could tell because he emitted his worst sounds outside Martin John's bedroom door as though he saved them up for him. Thus the sound of chronic tinkling each time Baldy Conscience shifted his neck would scupper his hole all right.

He has strong urges to pound Baldy Conscience, but he lacks the means to enact them and becomes distracted conjuring up scenarios of imagined humiliation for him, which only makes Martin John angrier because he realizes, as he concludes plotting each one, that he has still neither pounded him nor humiliated him. He is energized by thoughts of what he must do to Baldy Conscience and yet is stopped still in his tracks. That he cannot execute any active means to stop this man ruining his life or occupying his home. Never has he been so violently allergized to another human. Each and every time the Baldy Conscience moves or opens his mouth it inflicts an itchy discomforting plague on Martin John. Baldy Conscience is under his epidermis like scabies. Specks of him and his awfulness have lodged themselves into Martin John. Baldy is a new Cromwell for this South London landing.

⸱⸱⸱→

Martin John is sleeping less and less.

He is afraid of what Baldy Conscience is up to. That which he cannot see. He lays traps to monitor and track him. Mossad-type tricks. A piece of thread here. (Movement confirmed Baldy certainly uses the bathroom.) Markers on the teabags and the kettle. Again, he's stealing Martin John's teabags. He buys an extra lock for his room that he can secure from the inside and outside yet he's still convinced Baldy has been in and is moving things about. A deliberate taunting. He can see items appearing like that powder puff—how did that find its way into Martin John's room?

One Thursday Baldy Conscience returns a videotape to him which Martin John swipes hastily and disappears. He does not recall lending him it and a heightened panic lands that Baldy has breached his bedroom door and acquired the videotape from his intrusions. He opens the bedroom door again.

—Where did you get it?

—You lent it to me.

—I don't remember.

—You fookin gev it to me ya numpty.

Too many words, Baldy Conscience is releasing too many T-sounds and numpty doesn't sit well with him. These sounds are dementing. He must take cover from them. Under a blanket, moths and muck. But the voice volume increases and he can hear Baldy repeating fookin gev, fookin gev. Remember. Lent. Remember. Numpty, numpty, numpty.

Martin John does not want to look at Baldy Conscience anymore. When he sees him he squints, yet Baldy Conscience, bold as you like, holds his own and stares him down.

Startle-stares him down, nearly takes the underpants off him in that stare. He is out to destroy him. Baldy Conscience will take him down where the others until now have failed. Mam is right. They have come for him.

⋯→

He phones mam.

—They have come, he tells her. They are here. A man is here.

—Where are you Martin John? Are you in the pub? Put the head down and get on with it and stop with this nonsense. Don't be ringing me ever about no men. There's no men, she says. It's only women. Women you've to watch. Do ya hear me Martin John? Don't start again. For the love of God don't start again. I'm not for listening another word. I haven't the time or the patience.

⋯→

Martin John knows that Baldy Conscience set up the robbery which is why he's not giving you any details about the robbery because he knows that you'll take it back to Baldy Conscience first chance you get. You'll write it up here and there and you'll say this and hint at that and he won't have it. He won't have you sending Baldy Conscience to take a slice off him.

197

He is gathering evidence.

He is gathering evidence on Baldy Conscience before he makes his final move.

Evidence is what he's gathering. In order to gather evidence he needs the tools. The tools for evidence gathering are his work. Whatever you do now Martin John don't jeopardize the job or Baldy will come crumbling down on you.

⸺▸

More and more people are visiting Baldy Conscience in the house. It's hard to gather evidence with all these people.

The evidence is taking a while.

⸺▸

He examines Baldy Conscience's toothbrush and, using a set of tweezers, tries to find anything that will prove the theft of one of his biscuits. He buys a variety of biscuits, adds them to his tin marked Gaffney MJ. He scrawls a sign that reads *Landlord and Home Owner* on the back of the tin. He even places sticky tape on the bottom of the tin so he can monitor whether or not it has been moved. In a more inspired moment, and such moments join, breeze and buzz Martin John hourly, he imagines using Super Glue to adhere it to the shelf. He imagines Baldy having his arm ripped out of its socket and this image calms him down. Calms him to a place of satisfaction where he imagines that fucker suffering and it brings him peace.

The small cluttery house is getting taken over by young men wearing black donkey jackets and dark red Dr Marten boots. They're everywhere. They are stamping all over his life with their bloodied hooves. The house, which he has to remind himself he is in charge of, has become the Butlins Holiday Camp of Damp Indie Bands. Martin John wonders how they all fit up there in the bedroom. Every now and again, between the guitar bashing and worse than a bag of cats singing, he hears one of them thump, thump their boots down to his toilet. He tries to count based on these thumps how many men might be up there. Each time the door opens he can hear them laughing and the smoke seeps under his door downstairs.

⋯➔

The knock comes.
Martin John knows it's him. Doesn't answer.
The knock keeps coming.
And coming.
And coming.
He opens the door.
—Toilet's blocked.

Away he walks. Fortunately Baldy Conscience doesn't dally, for Martin John would have to lunge at him to save himself. For days Martin John has not been near his own bathroom. He has urinated into bottles and buckets and put them down the kitchen sink. Whoever has blocked the crapper up there it is one of the Radar Love boys. Now he must go up and face what the Butlin boys have done to his bathroom. He is terrorized in his own house. He fears the enemies. The infidels up on the landing. It's obvious Baldy

Conscience is dirty. He's probably infected and discharging. Martin John does not want to tread where he has trod, which becomes very challenging when they both share the same stairs, carpet and kitchen.

Martin John constructs and hangs a fallacious *Wet Paint* sign. He sticks it to the hallway wall and then, much further along, another, which reads *Paint Wet* and between the two a *Don't Tred Here* sign. He officiously adds a fourth notice that reads *Gaffney MJ, LANDLORD.* Since Baldy Conscience is a chancer he adds a *BLOCK CAPS BY ORDER* sign before the *Wet Paint, Don't Tred Here, Paint Wet, Gaffney MJ, LANDLORD.* Even though he is pleased with how it looks and wishes to remain and admire it longer, he forces himself out of the house because Baldy Conscience is stirring and he does not want that fuckface to come and sneer or he may just have to strangle him. Also, he has not fixed the toilet because he has no intention of fixing the toilet because, after all, Martin John is not even a fan of using the toilet to begin with. Mam told him to stop going upstairs.

⋯→

It's morning and he, Gaffney MJ, is thunderous.

The books he so carefully laid out in the hall to create two passages, in order to separate from Baldy Conscience's occupying plague, have been moved. Not just moved. Kicked. They form a toppled trail, zagging down the hallway. A correction has been added to the sign on the word Tred. TreAd it reads and his name has been changed to Daphney.

Worse, there's an ashtray in the middle of his kitchen table. This is the final desecration. He returns to his room and puts on a Flash Gordon video to try and calm his nerves so he might think. He must move on Baldy Conscience. He must do something. Because Baldy is crushing him.

⋯➔

One morning, Baldy Conscience enters the kitchen, throws open the window, pushes out the back door and says, It's too fucking dark and hot in here.

Martin John closes the door and lowers the window. He doesn't speak. He just infuses silence. He stands at the window with his hand keeping it firmly shut.

—Wha?

—It stays closed.

—Wha?

—It stays closed.

Strangely, Baldy retreats, boils the kettle, stabs his teabag and departs without a word. His ankles look angry.

Martin John has figured out he needs to be more terrifying. The more terrifying he is the more likely Baldy will repent.

He commences the labelling. Incessant labelling. Forensic labelling. He employs gaffer tape and a marker. Plus he purchases an identity stamp. It costs him 26 quid to have the rubber prepared with precisely the long-worded warning he wishes.

> If you remove or move this object or currently have this object in your hand you have violated code 1066.

Code 1066 sounds formal and legal. In fact it's the anniversary of the Battle of Hastings. One of the few dates that has stayed with Martin John. Oh 1066 he'll say, wasn't that 1066? Everything worth anything took place in 1066. Once he told mam he was in a 1066 type of situation. Shut up, she said. For the love of God, shut up with the numbers.

The warning, though rambling vague and rectangular, is stamped onto every copy of every newspaper, every cassette and every possession he has. He considers stamping it onto the cutlery, but the sticker would wash off and block the sink.

He labels his cloth bag in bold marker **GAFFNEY MJ SECURITY GUARD** until he notices people staring at him on the Tube and bus, and then he places his hand over the word **GUARD**. Only **SECURITY** is visible and it ensures he always has a seat empty either side of him.

He has learnt something has Martin John. He has learnt when people are afraid of you they move away, they move back, they back away off. They only need an inclination that you're someone to be afraid of. He sees now where he failed with Baldy Conscience. He did not establish that he was fearsome. He has not yet unnerved him. He will not do that again. In future he will be fearsome. He will display behaviour that is to be feared.

⇢

Martin John has a problem. And it's a sleep problem. All day, when he should be asleep after working the night shift, he's crouched in bed, attentive, listening for every squeak Baldy makes upstairs. Baldy's room is directly above him. Martin John's sleep is reduced to the two hours the BC sleeps in during the morning that coincide with Martin John knocking off his shift.

Increasingly he sleeps very little. This is not good. Things are not good when Martin John doesn't sleep. He's like a hunted mole, crouched behind the door, on edge of constant anxiety, jumping to at any ding. Even in the streets a piece of litter blowing ahead of him takes on startling proportions. Everything startles him. Everything startles him now that Baldy Conscience has his claws firmly inserted into his brain.

He worries a great deal about the nights does Martin John. The nights he's not in the house. He worries about what's happening and each morning he returns from work he carries a nagging fear that the Baldy Conscience will have burned the place down.

He worries a great deal about how much power the BC must know he has and what he might do with that power.

BC is undeterred. He is unaffected by Martin John's instructions and diligent labelling.

The ante must be upped.

The telephone is a great weapon.

The telephone is a great weapon in the battle with Baldy Conscience.

He knows the man works someplace. He has something of a job. He can't remember exactly what. Maybe it's cleaning he is. Is he a janitor? Does he clean drains? He rings every cleaning company listed in the telephone book and leaves threatening messages. Sometimes people answer. He reads aloud his threat with his mouth covered by a handkerchief. Sometimes the person simply answers *What?*

And so he must repeat his threat that if they employ a person by the name of "Baldy Conscience" terrible things will happen to their company, including the damaging of property and the endangering of human life.

He edited the threat speech a few times, to make it more concise and intimidating. It merely ends up sounding more and more formal and confusing to the phone responder.

—Wot?

—Who is this?

—I think you've got the wrong number.

—Are you fucking kidding me?

—Who is this?

—I think you've got the wrong number.

Once someone blew a whistle in his ear. He didn't like that.

Another time a woman said he'd already rung her because she also worked at another cleaning company.

The one that really scared him was the man who said his

number had flashed up and he knew where he lived and he was going to come over there to fucking burst him open and not clean up afterwards.

--->

Martin John does not like this woman.

He does not like this woman opposite him at the lunch table in the unit. He does not like what she is saying about Beirut.

She is saying she is from Beirut.

She is disputing what he says about Beirut.

She says there are no golden-shod women in Beirut.

She says the dogs are like dogs everywhere.

She says people are not always moving house in Beirut.

She repeats the word Beirut over and over again.

It's his word. His Beirut.

It's my Beirut, he says.

It's not your fucking Beirut, she says.

You've never been there, she says.

She says shite she doesn't know about.

Golden-shod, Martin John says.

Shut up.

I won't. Golden-shod.

You're crazy, she says.

--->

There was another such run-in with a woman on the bus. He cannot recall the number of the bus and this bothers him. He searches for the number. It's gone. Yet he knows it's there. In there, somewhere, amid the mass of worms gradually eating away at his various cortexes. In there is a number, it could be a single- or a double-digit or even a tri-ple-digit number. Was it an express? It could have been an airport bus. A double or a single-decker? His mind is seized with buses from two countries. Buses that have drivers with concrete feet that slam brakes suddenly and announce the destinations. Buses with ding-dong bells. Buses with no bells. Buses with smells. Buses with no smells. Bus hell.

Which bus was it? It's gone. Gone. The way it goes when he takes the drugs as they've told him to. Gradually more and more information being drained, pulled away—seep, seep, seep.

It began on the bus. The bus, Beirut and these women telling him what to do. The women telling him how it is. He has fought with women on buses before. There was the time, the other time, nothing to do with the Beirut time, that the woman accused him of treading on her ankle. Actually he'd been trying to rub against her leg. She didn't even have it right.

The woman shouted at him. Mam had not said no to the buses. Mam has said no to the Tube. Mam has said he's only to be on the buses in London. Mam has said. He doesn't remember what mam has said.

He phones her.
—What did you say?
—About what?
—About the buses?
—I didn't say anything about the buses.
—You did. Before.
—Before?
—Before.
Then he gives her a several-minute loop of before, before, before, before, before. She's gone then when he stops.

⋯➔

He phones her again.
—*Don't start*, she says.
—Don't be starting with me, Martin John. I haven't the patience. Did you take your tablets?

207

He's silent.

They're all after him with these tablets. In the tablets are the bus numbers, the bus colour, the bus shape. In the tablets are the golden-shod women that this unshod woman disputed. She, who is sitting here, in this dining room in the place they brought him because they said he didn't take his tablets. She who is wearing slippers. The way they are all wearing slippers in this ward.

⸺➤

The nurse offers him the tablet in a cup.

He says he doesn't like the colour of the cup. She says it's a colourless cup, but she'll see if there's any other.

She returns with another colour cup.

He says it's too big. He wants the tablet in a small cup. He says he won't read the *Daily Telegraph*. He says he wants the Beirut woman gone. The nurse says there's no Beirut woman. There's just Tonya. Tonya, it's Tonya, that's who it is. Tonya from Peckham. Tonya has a Walkman and is sat quiet. She has a magazine.

The next time the nurse returns, she brings four others with her and they inject Martin John in his flank or it might be his thigh. They certainly have him by the thigh. They push him flat on the bed to put the jab into him and in that pushing act they remind him how he likes to feel his bladder full. Bladder full against the mattress. He likes that he remembers. That is nice. Thank you he says to the five of them as they stream from his room. One person lifts his leg into bed and he stays there on his side. Just waiting. Waiting for he's not sure what: someone to lift his other leg?

⸺➤

Martin John can go home if he agrees to the team. The team will come and visit him. He agrees to the team without realizing that the team means a woman whose name begins with P. Patrice is his home care/mental health worker. He does not like words that begin with P so he will not answer the door to *atrice. Baldy Conscience answers the door to *atrice and says what he always says to anyone who comes to the door for anything, that he is the only person home and it is only he who lives in this house. He has heard Baldy Conscience say this before and back then he was alarmed. Now it is very convenient.

Each time *atrice returns, Baldy Conscience asks her questions. What does she want? Why is she calling? Baldy Conscience asks *atrice if she is his—Martin's—girlfriend. He has halved his name. Half-eradicated him in one question.

Is that why you want to know when the last time I saw him was? Martin John does not hear what *atrice says next but BC says Fuck you're kidding and Martin John does not like the sound of the you're kidding. The note in it is low. Too low. It's a deep-sounding word. Like Baldy Conscience is excited by what he has heard and he is going to do something with this information. Like erase his remaining half, the "Martin" in Martin John.

⇢

There were to be no P's. He had decided that when he made the lists of words from the *aper. He had seen the *roblems with P words and he was finished with them. That was how it would be. No P's.

⇢

He goes to visit Noanie so that if the hospital makes a fuss they will phone Noanie, who will say What harm? He was here. He is here. Noanie will say, What harm?

—You're here, she says. Where were you?
—I was there.
—You were.
—I was.
—Now I'm not there anymore.
—I see that. You're here.
—That's good. I'll tell her when she phones.
—Did she phone?
—Oh she did.
—When?
—Oh I don't know.
—It's a while since she phoned.

He bought Noanie a doughnut. Noanie cuts it in half.

When she eats her piece of the doughnut, Noanie shrivels her lip up and sucks at her teeth. It's the first time he notices her teeth are gone very bad.

—It's a long time since I had one of those, she says.

He brought the doughnut to make conversation. Now he is stuck with Noanie for the regimented three hours. He asks if they can watch the teletext on the television. You can. You can, she says. She has to do the washing-up and then she'll be in to him.

He brought me a doughnut and he watched the teletext. There could be nothing more normal than that, figures Martin John.

WHAT THEY KNOW:

The foot.

They found him by his foot.
He was removed to St Thomas' Hospital.
Knee abrasions.

⤑

Martin John has made mistakes.
When the fireman from the Lewisham Fire Brigade tugs him crudely by his ankles, Martin John remembers he has made mistakes.

Fucking hell, the fireman says.
That's how it is with Martin John.
That's how it was with Martin John.
And now, ever wary of firemen.

⤑

When the Lewisham Fire Brigade entered the home at 7 Cluny Place, which they described as an unremarkable South London mid-terraced dwelling in their paper report (two paper clips: they don't like them to come apart)— they faced a thick barrier of piled-up material.

Smoke. Someone called it in. There's a man living in that house. He hasn't seen him in months but he exists. *He's not all there, but he exists* was likely how the neighbour described him. He may have added harmless, weird, eccentric—kindly adjectives. Were they deserved? You'll decide amongst yourselves. As Martin John's mam says, We'll answer to the man who knows him best.

Someone called in a report of smoke.

They are still referring to him as The Occupant at this point.

—The Occupant fenced himself in.
—We don't know how he survived.

The firemen speculated that The Occupant would have suffocated if he hadn't been rescued. Martin John is irritated by such rescue stories. The firemen were an interruption.

Did you ask that fella being cut from the wreckage of the car; did you ask him if he wants to be saved? Martin John likes to shout at the television, at innocuous radio reports that mention the word: firemen. He does not like cat-rescue stories either. He gets that from mam. For the love of God, she'll say, there is sometimes a very good reason a cat goes up a tree. It's the only thing they agree on. Cats go up trees for a reason: don't go up after them. Martin John does not have a cat. He does not have a cat because he doesn't want people going up trees after his cat. He cannot guarantee that people will not go up trees.

Also, he does not like cameras on bridges. If a man or woman wants to go over the side of a bridge, for the love of God let them go peacefully. He does not believe that people who go off bridges can be saved. He believes it's reasonable to want to go over the side of a bridge. He does not believe people fundamentally change. He has struggled with this himself. Has he tried? We do not know. There are some things we aren't going to know about Martin John. He may have concluded people can't change because he tried to change, or he may have concluded it because he cannot be bothered to find out, preferring to cave in to his urges rather than heed the instruction he cease with them. Or it may be Baldy Conscience who forced him to conclude this.

215

He doesn't do well with interruption.

We know that about him. We've learnt that about him. We have swallowed it. We accept this about him.

We do not accept his other stuff. The behaviour, the girl—did he, didn't he? Would he, wouldn't he? Would you or wouldn't you if you were his mother?

⋯→

We found it hard to believe someone could be living there, the firemen said in the official kind of places firemen say such things: into each others' ears, into a camera, into a phone. It's the heavy boots that make them confess. That pull their conscience to the ground.

You aren't allowed to dislike firemen. There's a law against it. They'll save your life, even if you don't want saving. *Ssssh*. That's Martin John speaking.

Would there be a reason why a man might not want saving? Could that reason be as simple as not wanting to visit someone on a Wednesday? Would you accept that?

⋯→

Someone's in there.

Fuck off.

Serious, someone's in there.

⤍

It was thick, thick with papers, boxes. *Crap* one man called it. *Place is full of crap.* Can't see anything except crap. Just crap, crap, crap. Nothing here but crap. Smouldering, toppling, moulding, indescribable crap. Crap, crap, crap. We called out. We were ready to give up when Ted here remained convinced there might be someone in there. I was convinced, Ted says.

Martin John has noticed they used the words thick and convinced twice. Did you notice that? They are speaking very formally for firemen, except for the fuck off. It's the camera and the newspaper quotes that do it. They are on the hose ready for the quotes. Martin John has seen this. He's been around cameras in his job. He has a relationship with the papers. And now we're back to Ted.

Ted shuffles forward as the other men back off. He shuffles forward to have his moment. Usually firemen have monosyllabic football-player moments. Not Ted. This is his situation. He found the foot. He tugged it. It's his foot now.

—I saw his foot first. When I saw the foot I knew we had him.

—Did he call out?

Here come the questions.

—Not really. To be honest I thought he might actually not wanna be found. He made so little noise. But that's sometimes how these *cases* are.

These cases?

Martin John is incredulous.

He didn't become a case until later on.

217

Ted has it wrong.

But he's lying here on this stretcher facing a diagnosis of severe knee abrasions.

⋯→

Martin John was not a case until the Chair. When mam put him in the Chair and he removed himself from the Chair that time, then he became A Case. It's important we maintain the correct timeline here. Martin John is on to us.

I wasn't a case at that point, he rages.

Chronology is important to him.

He wants it in sequence. But it won't be told in sequence because these things never happen in a sequence, do they now Martin John?

If you ask him anything directly he will go quiet, retreat. Did you do it? Did you touch her? Who else did you touch?

See, he's gone quiet.

⋯→

The one fireman asks the other fireman *how many years*?

How many years do you think it takes to make this mess?

The other fireman is not listening because he's thinking about having a wank.

That is not necessarily a fireman thing. Except Martin John believes it is. They are masturbators, chronic with their hoses. If that fireman had not been in such a hurry to get home to attend to himself, Martin John believes he never would have persevered and believed someone was within, in the house. See how the sequence troubles him? See how he knows things are controlled? See? See? See?

Yet he doesn't see.

Go back to our first question. Rewind.

Did you do it Martin John? He'll give you nothing. He's

218

got nothing. *I got nothing. I got nothing.* We've got nothing on him. Except the women. The women don't feel this way.

Ask them.

If you can find them.

They are among you.

⋯➔

Every time there's a case like this, the one fireman asks the other fireman: Why do they do it? How does it happen? Doesn't anybody know about them? Imagine your mother finding you living like this?

It's a problem. The other fireman tells the first fireman he thinks too much. The other fireman primarily thinks about one thing. It keeps things simple. We aren't fucking social workers, *are* we?

He feels a bulge in his pants on the *are.*

Martin John would find that suspicious. A man having an erection on the verb to be, and at a question too. He would find that suspicious. He wouldn't appreciate it in a cross-word clue. So you should know that. You should know the things he does and doesn't appreciate, if we are going to carry on with this. If not—well, hang up now, as the operator would say.

That's aggressive, but you see this hasn't been an easy book for any of us.

⋯➔

Withdraw the case, mam said. Don't go ahead with it. He's a sick man now. He's completely out of his mind and no danger to anyone.

I guarantee you he's no danger. I have him secured, she said. He won't bother you again. Withdraw the case, she said.

There's no need to go after him.

219

This was mam rehearsing. She rehearsed what to say when they came for him. They'd come yet, surely they would. There have been hints sufficient.

⋯→

Years ago his mother had come. His mother came and asked that she—The Girl—not press charges. She, his mother, said The Boy, her son, would be going away and promised he would never bother her again.

⋯→

—Did he bother you again?

—That's not the point.

—You are about to take a man, who's half-fried in the head, and put him on the stands. Is that what you want?

—Come in, The Girl who is now a woman with girls of her own, said. Come in, she said to the Jack Russell dog who'd slipped out between their legs when she'd answered the door.

—There were others, she said as she shut the door.

⋯→

It's money they are after. It's money they want.

—If it's money you're after, he hasn't any. Like I said he's half-fried in the head and can barely hold a job.

It would be years again before she'd offer her this explanation.

WHAT THEY DON'T KNOW:

It put me in the Chair.

Martin John now has conversations about what took place and the how and the where of it almost daily. He battles it out in the air in front of him and between his two hands— slapping facts between his two hands like another might slam pizza dough.

I wasn't a case then—slap.

I became a case later—slap.

I am a case now—slap.

I hate the way these firemen rush everything—slap.

They want to put/pull everything out—slap.

They don't want anything to go in for the slow burn—slap.

I never trust the likes of them—slap.

But do they ever mop up the water?—slap.

Where does the water go?—slap.

He beats the facts aloud and about for the truth, while in his imagination people, God's people, the other pedestrians, give way on the pavement or cross the road or move aside at Euston Station to avoid him.

Sometimes mam calls out to him in the Chair to *stop making that racket would ya.*

⋯➔

Ted the Fireman has said too much, he has exceeded the newsbyte. We're back to the official spokesperson and moving on to tomorrow's weather forecast, which includes the word disappointing; people may be disappointed by this week's weather. The prediction is for disappointment.

⋯➔

This was the first time Martin John was (officially) introduced to the public. They met him foot-first. But it was in Beirut he made his mark.

Yet there was stuff, that stuff, all that stuff, that weird kind of stuff, that happened before Beirut.

⋯→

The Foot,
The Kettle,
The Chair.
The Foot,
The Kettle,
The Chair.
The Chair,
The Kettle,
The Foot.
The Kettle,
The Groin,
The Pain.
Mam. Mam. Mam.

⋯→

The ward,
The ward.
The ward.
The burn,
The pain,
The burn.
The query, the query, the query.
The Chair,
The bed,
The query.
The tongue,
The lips,
The mouth.
Shut up, shut up, shut up.

⋯→

WHAT THEY DON'T KNOW:

Noanie told her to tie him up.

Noanie has her home and it is to this home that mam has instructed Martin John to go every Wednesday, whether it suits him or not. Now Noanie has sent word to say he failed to arrive at her home the last several Wednesdays. A letter has been writ to mam to tell her this. A letter written that paused itself over a few days to say *if he doesn't come tomorrow again I will post thi*s and thus several Wednesdays have passed since its writing.

How many ways were there to say: Get Out and Visit Noanie on a Wednesday? Mam was unequivocal. He had to visit each Wednesday. She didn't care what time he visited. He could visit at 6 am or 6 pm or somewhere in between, but he could not fail to visit Noanie. This was the agreement.

How many ways are there to say? *We don't care what suits you Martin John. Get out and visit Noanie.*

⋯➤

Martin John is no longer respecting The Agreement. The only possible explanation is Martin John must be being held against his will. Had she not spelled out how strongly he was to respect The Agreement?

Noanie understood. Noanie said *these types of men*. Men like Martin John needed *locking up* or perhaps she lessened it to *tying up* once mam gave her a look. Like you would a goat, Noanie stated. You tie them up so they can't eat beyond the boundaries of what they should be eating. You have to contain them. There's a point they pass where there's no stopping them, there's no helping them, nothing. Like drinkers, she assures mam.

—Is he past it, do you think?

—Oh he's long past, says Noanie.

—That's why, Noanie says, we had The Arrangement.

The Arrangement, like you know, that he was to come here every Wednesday.

Noanie was telling her it was time to tie him up. It was time to lock him up. Noanie was telling her she'd had enough. If Noanie had had enough it was time to pack him up. For Noanie was the most reliable among them. Every Wednesday she was to be found behind that front door, which is more than can be said for some people.

⋯➔

WHAT THEY DON'T KNOW:

Hoarding in.

In the matter of hoarding in, Martin John had to make sombre preparations. He did not just click his fingers and mounds of crap appeared. He had to move the crap into place. It had to lend itself to strategic battle. There were three levels of preparation that would usually have taken place over several months or years even.

Such preparations would exhaust the ordinary-thinking man. But Martin John is no ordinary-thinking man, rather he is a man being raced and traced by a planet of Meddlers, all under the guidance of Baldy Conscience.

He is trying to defeat someone living on top of his head.

Customarily your enemies are at a distance, where a trench and an eyeline are possible. Not here. Not for Martin John.

Martin John was the horse on the final furlong with a wobbly ankle who thundered on nonetheless because his jockey rode him high and horses are not prone to reverse.

⋯➔

In the matter of correcting the mess he has made Martin John is either unequivocally unaware he has created mess or unequivocally not bothered by the prospect of furthering his mess.

⋯➔

Then he rang the police and said he wished to *anonymously* report a man he believed to be bothering women. Martin John had seen him on the Tube.

Then he rang the police to report *anonymously* a man who was stealing from parking meters in Soho.

He filed a long list of reports from different phone boxes and each time he gave a very, very precise description of Baldy Conscience, including the hat and shoes he had seen him wearing yesterday.

Finally, he rang the police again and reported he had now seen exactly where the man lived and gave them his home address.

...→

Nuisance calls.
Nuisance calls the police said when they rammed on his door.
Stop making these nuisance calls.
It was a warning they told him.
A warning to stack up with the other warnings.
Now 3 warnings in total.
Warnings needed company.
Did a South London warning have the same power as a North London warning?

...→

If mam said they would come after him for the things he had done, he had only to pass along these same things to Baldy Conscience and surely they'd pursue him in the same manner.

It's a plan. Martin John thinks he has a plan. He has made mistakes but now there's a plan.

WHAT THEY DON'T KNOW:

She ties him into a chair.

He did not fight me over it. Ever. He never questioned it. Just let me tie him in when I left the house.

We carried along that way for a while and he made no protest. I thought we had settled it. This was how it had to be. Sure he knew that himself.

--->

WHAT THEY DON'T KNOW:

The circuits.

The circuits were gone once Euston was gone.
There was never another circuit to be done or had or seen once Euston Station was closed to him.
He missed the circuits.
He went to the tracks for the circuits.

⋯→

Never once did he say to me: What are you doing? Why are you doing this? Martin John was passive. It mighta been the only time he was passive. He made it easy on me.

⋯→

Mam ties him in the Chair so that he can't go to the toilet.
To make his bladder full again.
More pronounced.
It was thoughtful of her. Kind.
This is what Martin John thinks when she ties him in.

WHAT THEY DON'T KNOW:

Pots, pots pots.

All mam's worries live inside a teapot. One settlement within a colony of teapots. She has written them on pieces of paper, backs of receipts, parts of used envelopes—all tightly folded and pressed deep into the teapot.

The colony of teapots holds decades of anxieties. She calls each one Pot. Pot usually lives in a hard-to-reach spot, with a booklet or expired calendar stuck in front of him so suspicion will not be aroused, nor will she be tempted to overstuff him. Some of the notes contain dates/times of phone calls or things people have muttered in passing about Martin John. Or that which she suspects they want to ask beyond, How is he getting on in England? The odd prayer or quote lifted from the radio are also slid in. Often the quotes are from dead American presidents. There may be one in there from Einstein or Aristotle. One is from a mechanic, Joe, who gave instructions on what indicated your engine was failing during a Midwest radio phone-in.

Today she will write what will be the final note before she seals this teapot closed with strong tape. There are approximately 11 other pots, full and retired to the top cupboard not far from her bed, so in the event of a fire she might nab a couple and exit. But their population is grown too large now for the quick removal she intended. It has gone on too long. Even if there were a fire, would she even remove herself? Or might she simply burn alongside them?

Each lid has been taped closed and she can track the changes in tape down the years. How she chose thicker tape that year. Or used insufficient tape or tape that didn't altogether facilitate the level of deteriorating dampness in her house. She hasn't any emotional attachment to the teapots themselves. They are mere random ones that came her way.

here aren't so many details on what Martin John xactly and precisely did at an obscure railway station in ertfordshire, England, but it is supposed by mam he was siting Noanie or on his way home from visiting her when happened.

hatever he did—and mam suspects some kind of expo- e or tip slip because of his proximity to the litter bin led to his removal to hospital where the phone calls ommenced.

at did you do? mam asks him before squealing twice as d, *I don't want to know. Save me from it, d'ya hear? Get rself out of there. Get yourself out of there. Get out and visit nie on Wednesday.*

One year she used a stainless steel one, but never again. She hated the idea she could accidentally catch the light or a glimpse of something in the side of it. It also gave her memories of very bad tea brewed in such teapots at weddings and funerals. Since life was a daily funeral, she didn't turn out for many of them. She only went to funer-als where she suspected the person had a good reason to have a grudge against her on account of Martin John. She knew that her absence would suggest guilt.

She always took communion at those funerals and she attended every stage of the mourning. She could imagine a slim crowd at her own funeral. She could see Martin John going to the grave with no one at his funeral. They might go together and make it easy on all.

But her thoughts are now disordered. She has a final note to place inside this grubby-looking teapot and she has to seal it closed. She won't open another teapot this way she decides. That's it for the *pot, pot, pots* as she calls them.

After she put Martin John in the Chair she knew there was no further use for the teapots. What would you be doing firing things into them after that? Ask yourself.

···→

WHAT THEY KNOW:

The railway stations.

WHAT THEY DON'T KNOW:

Euston.

Martin John was technically chased out of Euston Station by the oppressive forces of police and observant railway workers. He was forced further down the train line. They made him hop a few platforms away.

If they hadn't chased him away from his beloved Euston station he never would have given the people of a somnambulant Welwyn North train station the fright they claimed he did.

A man in the car park, heading home to his bungalow with climbing magnolia on his mind, swore when he phoned him in that Martin John was tipping his nib towards a rubbish bin. That he saw him with his trousers open.

We've not long even had rubbish bins restored to the station, he complained, muttering about the IRA. I knew he was near the rubbish bin because yesterday I slipped my own sweet wrapper in it.

WHAT THEY DON'T KNOW:

The railway stations.

Martin John has routines. He calls the railway announcer's recorded voice Molly or Annie depending on that station. Mainly he's at Euston, where she is Annie. Annie speaks every few seconds. She speaks to him. She's attentive, is Annie.

"The train standing at Platform 2 is the …"
"Please keep your belongings with you at all times. Unattended luggage could be removed and destroyed or damaged."

Martin John has a relationship with Annie. He brings his notebook. Usually starts doing a line with Annie once he's finished the crossword and the letters page. He does not like his news people, his word people and his train people to hover too close to each other.

Sometimes it distresses him to choose between Annie and the crossword, but Martin John has rules.

Don't look at them direct.

Move in swift and out even swifter.

Don't be greedy.

Bare flesh is dangerous.

A brush is but a brush.

Press up against her in queues. Quick. Hard. Into the hips. And out. 3 seconds.

When they give you the look—that look—by return, offer no look.

Even if they shout, stay calm and continue to write down Annie's words sailing over their mutually distressed heads.

Mutually distressed?

Well yes, for if he's interrupted then it's not a ritual. If he's interrupted, if he does not complete the brush or flash or rub, a circuit has been interrupted. If a circuit is lost he must calculate the probable impact of this.

BAD THINGS MAY HAPPEN.

Bad things may happen to the person passing. To the woman he failed to make contact with or to the person walking in the other direction.

In order to repair a bad circuit, he has to make a number of further circuits. When he makes continuous circuits the passengers, their luggage, their flow, interrupts him. Also, when he makes continuous circuits staff notice him, walkie-talkies are raised and the circuits have to speed up. He has been lifted from his circuits. That's a fact.

WHAT THEY KNOW:

Mam.

Mam does not like the new talk. The new talk about Beirut. The talk he brought home from London. Mam does not like the new talk about Beirut that he won't stop with. Dogs, women, heat, hills, entwined with weddings and daughters. He'd been blaguarding a bit about Beirut before, but now he's gone away off into an entirely new gabbling orbit. He is driving her spare.

What are you saying? What are you saying?
Would ya stop!
What are you on about? You don't have any children, never mind four daughters married in Beirut.
You'll have the pair of us locked up if you carry on this way.

This was the gentler spot she started in.

Shut up.
Shut up.
Shut up.
Would ya
SHUT UP.
For God's sake, shut up about Beirut. If I hear the word Beirut again I'll hand you over.

I've enough. I've enough of it. I'm not for listening another word. It's enough to drive a body to drink.

And still yet on he sang.
Beirut, Beirut, can you hear me Beirut?

Along with his other sin-cervating ramble about the rain and the harm and on and on, he scrolls out these sermons to himself and anyone unfortunate enough to be in listening distance. Finally she pushes a set of earplugs into his ears hoping the constant drone of himself unto himself might deliver him to a full stop.

Martin John believes mam is in league with Baldy Conscience and that's why she's telling him *shut up, shut up, shut up* every time he mentions Baldy or Beirut. She is very bothered by Beirut. Hot and bothered, yet no hills for her.

Baldy Conscience has succeeded. He has overthrown them. He is here with Martin John. Back here, in the back bedroom, where every backward fellow must dwell.
    Martin John has a plan.
    A plan to catapult himself from all this though.
    Most backward fellas don't have a plan.
    They just stay put.

---→

She tied him in. Mam tied him in the Chair for a reason she did not specify. She did not specify the reason because she had been told not to. We know who told her to tie him in. We don't need to say it aloud. Martin John is watching us. His ears are open. If we say it aloud he may make ugly screaming noises and accuse us of things.
    As soon as things are said aloud, accusations fly.

251

⟶

She tied him in, and it wasn't too bad being tied in, not as bad as the newspapers might later speculate, but remember Martin John is ahead of the newspapers. He has studied them. He understands their consciousness. He knows how their columnists tick. Bin changes, wine glasses, poll tax, landlord wars and gilpy Jesus Janey freakery. He is ahead of them, but we are alongside him now. Pad, pad, pant, pant.

They'd label a man like him troubled. P words might be used. "In quotes though," as a by-product of someone else's mouth. Someone certainly fed by Baldy Conscience. Someone who said something aloud and now the accusations are in print.

⟶

He needed to reach a telephone. He must report Baldy Conscience. God knows the damage the man would have done to the house and to the others who had failed to meet Baldy Conscience's demands.

Martin John could see a long line of them all under Baldy's direction, wearing rain macs, all reporting to Baldy, all except those in Beirut, those who had the strength, width and wherewithal to withstand him. To resist Baldy's summons, his lies, his domestic occupation and chronic borrowing of other people's precious newspapers. They stood beside Martin John. It was only in Beirut he'd survive. Baldy Conscience could never take on the lads in Beirut. Except which lads? Which lads was he thinking of? Was it the green lads? Was it random lads? Was it lads he'd seen on the telly or on a poster? Any lad, any lad in Beirut would do, any lad in Beirut could tackle Baldy Conscience.

He needed to get to a phone. Mam was cute about the phone. Since *that* time he made *them* calls. It was *them* calls that she tied him in for. He remembers now.

He would have to be out of the Chair in order to reach a phone.

⋯→

⟶

The roar.
Outta him.
Still he kept pouring.
The yelping.
Outta him.
Even as she tried to grab the kettle.
Tight
on
he held.
Then pushed the spout into his groin and poured hard.
She didn't like his eyes or the sound of him during it.
Obviously.

⟶

WHAT THEY DON'T KNOW:

When he had it done.

He stood. He held the empty kettle and he howled and he howled and he howled. He bowelled in them howls meticulously, and she couldn't understand how he could still hold the kettle so tight with all that growling noise coming out of him.

If he'd used the electric kettle it coulda been worse, she would later observe to the doctors.

He used the kettle that sat on the edge of the range. A chronically on-the-boil broiling kettle. The one she used for pouring hot water into dirty stuff that she wouldn't put her good kettle near.

⋯➔

She did not take the trousers off him.
She left him in them for a very good reason.
You left them in their own puddles.
Puddles of their own creating.
She put him in the car and drove him to the hospital.
He was strangely quiet.
It's a crime scene, she thought.

⋯➔

At the hospital she handed him over.
    He told them only about Beirut and needing to get to a wedding.

⋯➔

Later she had to tell them the facts: *he poured a hot kettle down on himself like y'know*. She nodded her head in emphasis as she said it like they may have entirely missed the reason why he was here.

—Was it an accident?

—It was no accident, she said. He held the kettle tight. I couldn't get near it. He held it like a gun and then scalded it into himself backwards.

⋯→

They took him in straight away.

She washed her hands.

She washed her hands again.

As she pulled the paper towel from its holder she thought of the many times she had considered he was not right in the head and she thought that it was perhaps a surprise he hadn't done it sooner and she wondered exactly when had he planned it? She wondered if he would tell the doctors that she tied him in the Chair and she felt confident that the doctors would agree with her reasons for doing so. What else could you do? And together they would all nod in agreement.

⋯→

Only once did Martin John make a comment when she tied him in. It wasn't even a comment as much as an observation.

—What if there's a fire?

—There's one fella here who'll start a fire and it's you. You are in this chair, so there will never be a fire.

She always talked through what she was doing while she tied him in. As she pulled the rope, she'd ask, *is that too tight? We don't want it to hurt you. We only want to keep you safe*. Sometimes she turned on the telly for him. Asked him which channel he wanted. Sometimes he replied and sometimes he didn't. She chose the channel that would excite him the least and went to work.

Of course she went to work. She had to work. How else would she have kept them fed? It was cleaning work, lots of hard mopping. Often when her shoulders pained, she knew it was atonement for all the hurt her body had inadvertently created. She would pray as she mopped, but she would never say the Hail Mary. She would pray in sayings. *Let him who has not sinned cast the first stone. Passion of Christ, strengthen me. Kind Jesus, hear my prayer. Hide me within your wounds. Immaculate Heart of Mary. Pray for us. St Joseph. Pray for us. St John the Evangelist. Pray for us.* Then she puzzled over how St John the Evangelist had ever snuck onto her list as she squeezed out the mop. But every time he was there. Every incantation he turned up. She couldn't rid her tongue of the man.

Martin John needed no details of her work. Only that she must go out now for a while but would be back soon enough. He was dangerous when he got information. Any small bit could set him off. It had, she reasoned, taken years to restrain him safely in the Chair. She was only doing what the doctors and those in authority refused to do. She was only doing what needed to be done with bad men. Bad men aren't good for us, she thought, resigned, the way you're probably thinking about how long this is taking to read or how uncomfortable that chair is. Say it. Say it now. It's uncomfortable. Time to shift the cushions behind your back.

⋯➔

She went to the hospital canteen and ate a very large tuna sandwich. She was never a fan of tuna and would not be making a habit of it. It wasn't the sort of thing that appealed to her, the smell alone, but she needed to be ready for the questions. The police might be involved. Surely they'd all come now. They were probably waiting upstairs.

⇢

There was no sign of the guards when she returned upstairs.
Maybe the police were sorting out paperwork.

⇢

She contemplates using the word depraved to describe him,
but stops short. She can't be sure. Is he honestly depraved,
or simply raving?
    Is there any difference?

⇢

If she no longer has to deal with Martin John (if they lock
him up in here or wherever it is they lock these people up),
would she be able to go for her lunch or dinner now and
again to Dunnes Stores? She thought of the Carvery deal
where they give you a few vegetables and mash potatoes
along with a slice of beef or a bit of chicken.

⇢

The doctor seemed surprised when she inquired about castration. She did not mess about, just came out with it.
    —Do you castrate fellas like him? Is that what you do?

He said he was a burns doctor and they'd be moving Martin
John to the Burns Unit.
    Mam assumes him a Junior. They know nothing. They
haven't a clue and are just reporting to the fellas above
them. He was being coy.

⇢

—Have they been in yet? she asked the Junior.

—Who?

—Who else? The Guards.

—I don't think so, the doctor said.

—If he used the electric kettle it coulda been worse.

He did not say anything further to her after that. He has been told not to initiate any conversation. To keep the crime scene preserved, if you like, not to contaminate the evidence or complicate things, she assumed.

···→

Finally the psychiatric people came. You took a while, she said.

We understand there are some issues, they said.

We'll wait for the guards, she told them warmly. I don't want to have to repeat myself.

···→

The psychiatric people added another woman. As if we need an interpreter, she thought, but things were bad enough and she didn't want more time to be added to whatever sentence he would be facing.

The psychiatry people did not wait for the guards though. They asked her questions.

She asked them questions. The same question she'd asked the other fella.

Would castration be an option?

···→

—How long has he not been himself?

—It's about thirty-five years since he was absolutely normal, she confirms flatly.

—Thirty-five years?

WHAT THEY DON'T KNOW:

What the doctor said.

—That's right.

—And has he been in hospital before?

—Oh God no, no no. Never before, doctor. I wouldn't let them near him.

—And what was it that made you bring him up today?

—Oh he's taken very bad doctor.

—How has he taken bad?

—The things he's doing.

—What's he doing?

—I'd rather not say.

—OK. What's he doing that he doesn't usually do?

—He's not speaking sense doctor. He hasn't said a proper word, just old gabble.

—How long is it since he spoke?

—Ah it must be going on four months.

—Four months?

—Whatever you gave him before when he was here with ye stopped him speaking.

—So he has been in hospital before?

—Oh he has, but it wasn't me who put him there. Only for what he done I never would have brought him today.

—Who was it brought him in the last time?

—I forget now. One of the shops, the security, and in London he was never outta the hospital. He's much worse doctor, much worse this time.

—How has he deteriorated?

—I'd rather not say, but he poured the kettle all over his trousers. He probably wanted to get a stain out of the trousers, she adds as an afterthought.

But the doctor isn't listening.

—So you witnessed it?

⸺⟶

The doctor exits the least comprehensive interview with a family member of his career and nods to another.

—Nothing doing, he says. We'll have to have his hearing tested to rule out mutism.

WHAT THEY DON'T KNOW:

She (Our Woman) is here.

Martin John is in his hospital bed and opposite is a new woman who wants only to hear about Beirut. He has found her. They lie on corresponding sides of the ward and exchange words throughout the day and night on an ever circling/recycling loop. Beirut and the dogs and the shoes and the women and the bread and Beirut and back.

It's lovely, he thinks. And then it ends.

⸱⸱⸱→

She does come back. The woman. And she goes again or maybe it is that he goes? Somebody goes.

His mother comes back, but her visits are interrupted by all the travel required. Mam leans down to his ear by the blanket and hisses.

—*You're a filthy creep.*

She may or may not have said they were going to execute him. It was hard to hear because someone down the ward was yelling and that bed over there with the yeller was suddenly surrounded.

⸱⸱⸱→

The woman in the bed opposite is brilliant. She shouts that mam is trying to kill him.

One night she crawls in beside him.
Her feet aren't even cold.
They lie there. He rigid.
They stare up. They don't look at each other.
Really.

⋯→

Her feet are not cold because she is wearing socks.
A nurse discovers her.
I wasn't here, I wasn't there, she says.
Neither here nor there is where she was.
Martin John keeps his eyes shut.
Until it passes.

He doesn't like Meddlers.
The nurse smells like a Meddler.
The woman was only visiting is all.
Was it strange?
It mighta been.

⋯→

The visiting woman is stirring Meddlers.

Martin John does not like Meddlers.
He moves a pillow to the side of each ear like barricades to
keep the Meddlers back.
How to keep the woman back who brings the Meddlers?

⋯→

The next time the woman opposite visits him in his bed it
is even stranger. Very strange altogether.
    He doesn't like it.

—Nurse, nurse, she's in my bed, he shouts. Get her out.

—What are you shouting about? the nurse says.

—Get her out, he says.

—There's no one in your bed. Stop, would you, before you wake the other patients.

The nurse says if he isn't going to go to sleep, she's going to have to put him to sleep. Or did he mishear her?

⋯→

Martin John, again, finds the woman opposite him on the ward in his bed.

—There isn't enough room, he protests.

Nonetheless she rolls in beside him, shoving him over.

She asks him questions this time.

Questions he is tired of answering.

She is very interested in Beirut.

Perhaps a bit too interested.

We don't know yet, he thinks. We don't know what way she's going to go. We don't know whom she may be in touch with.

⋯→

He doesn't answer.

She calls out again.

Can you hear me Beirut?

⋯→

The woman across from him is brilliant.

The problem is she attracts Meddlers.

She is brilliant until she visits him in bed.

Until she attracts Meddlers.

Martin John does not like Meddlers.

He has made mistakes.

But he has never liked Meddlers.

That's a fact.

⋯→

The woman in the opposite bed must stop bringing Meddlers.

Her Meddlers are a problem.

Martin John tells her this.

Very loudly.

He tells her this after she has told mam she is going to kill her for the way she's treating Martin John.

Mam is very nervous and leaves the ward.

People surround the bed.

Both beds.

She has done it now, Martin John thinks.

She had brought Meddler Bedlam upon them.

She has brought Meddlers to their pillows and to peer inside their eye sockets. He can't help her now, he thinks.

She's gone too far.

She's too far gone.

⋯→

Martin John is removing his pyjama bottoms and walking about the ward with only his top on, allowing his bits to be wobbly and loose below.

At first the other patients suggest he's forgotten his trousers. Then the man in the bed who once went to Spain says, Put your fucking trousers on, I don't want to look at your cock.

WHAT THEY KNOW:

Where they found him.

"Mate, you alright?" Silence.

The police have a problem. The suspect lies curled below, by the wheels of the train, wrapped around them. They can only see the back of his head and neck. His legs are under the carriage.

Who let him down there?

How to get him up?

WHAT THEY DON'T KNOW:

How did he get down there?

"Mate you can't be down there. So I need you to come up."
Silence.
"If you are not going to come up we'll have to come down and get you."

···→

Martin John has wedged himself, somehow, no one watching entirely sure how, below on the track by the train wheels. He looks to be underneath the train, but a part of him is showing. Enough to indicate: A man is down here.

···→

"Mate, can you hear me? If you can hear me, wave your hand."
Silence.
For Martin John, where there are police there may also be firemen.

···→

The police are gathering pace, unrolling Tactic Number Two.
"There are a lot of people on this train who want to get to Wales to catch a boat. The longer you stay down there the more likely they'll miss it."

Silence.
He's lying. The copper is lying. Martin John knows you have to change in Nuneaton. What sort of an eejit do they take him to be? The only prick that wouldn't know that would be Baldy Conscience. Baldy probably told them that Martin John's a simple fella, maybe a backward fella. Maybe a fella who doesn't know stuff, the sorta fella who watches the Eurovision. He knows stuff. He knows things that you don't even know. He knows the fucken train time-tables backwards.

274

⋯→

The police seem to think Martin John is making a suicide pitch.

He is making no such thing.

He is down here because his circuits were interrupted.

He is down here because they have not taken his charges against Baldy Conscience seriously.

He is down here because he is fed up with the metal bedside table in the hospital ward, where they have been keeping him since the firemen, knee abrasions and the tip-slip.

But most of all he is down here on account of that nun he met 15 minutes ago, and it did not work out well between the two of them. It's the nun's fault.

There's some confusion over Baldy Conscience being the nun. They are not clever, these police officers. I mean, how, with her habit, would you even begin to tell if a nun was a Baldy Conscience?

They tell him the nun is gone. It's safe for him to come up now.

They don't know exactly where. But this man Lee here swears she's gone.

They always tell you their names when they are lying to you.
They always tell you they are just like you.
They are not.
They always tell you they know how you feel.
They do not.
They do this.
It's what they do.
What they are paid to do.

Lee, though, says he's looked the entire station over and there are no nuns. If there were one, Lee would see her. If there was one before, she is gone. She's probably gone on a train.

"Give us your hand. We need you to come back up. I'll give you a hand up. Just move away from the wheels and come over here."

Silence.

···→

Martin John had his domain and his territory organized. He'd lain his napkins out across the table. 4 x 4. He had his tea—teabag still in cup—and it was only upon its removal and his strange dunking routine, where he anoints every corner of the table (wherever he sits), that he caught her attention and she is the reason he is down here now.

Sort of.

Not exactly.

See, she chastised him.

Just a look. But it was enough. He's been here before with them. He does not like those *authority looks* that nuns and not just nuns, but also women, can give. He has a bit of a history and a backlog of them. He's gotten them on buses, on the Tube, on escalators and in queues. There was one that caused quite a bit of trouble; she made loud ugly noises in his face and tried to scratch him.

He also noticed the nun's leg, her brown, stocking-wrapped leg, strapped into, if not imprisoned inside, shoes you would put on a horse. Everything from the sternness up top to the rigidity down below set him off. He had not even looked at her face. He had not even said hello to her the way he was trained to do. To acknowledge it's either hell or hello there Sister. How were you even meant to make contact properly with the bride of Christ?

You were not to be sitting here with your fat bladder paddling itself and appealing for the release Mother Nature expected when she formed it inside you. You were not to be eating overpriced dry scones and flat fizzy drinks that were going to give you a heart attack and make you want to piss stronger, louder and forever. The normal and natural and necessary thing to do was ask *And where are you on your way to today, Sister?* The normal, natural and necessary thing to do was to act normal and natural rather than dolloping your tea bag *über alles*. This was especially necessary when, like Martin John, you're wearing a hospital-issued green gown and you forgot to take your coat when you left the building during a moment that wasn't supposed to happen.

And yet they do happen.

Martin John is offered these moments.

Here is one now.

Like every other moment where the flesh of a woman had been within his reach, Martin John does not demonstrate much that would make any woman entirely comfortable sitting beside him. Women have to have their flesh around Martin John and they must accept, unbeknownst, it's going to be difficult for them if they are in reaching distance. Except this woman is a nun and she's trained in accepting unaccept-able people and making them accept certain things in her presence. She has a stern social contract in her footwear and eyewear. She's no messer. She means business. The business of retreat from the greedy valley of man and unto the restorative replenishment of Christ. She eats brown rye crackers. She has her own flask of tea. And, no thank you, she would not like to share Martin John's teabag that he's bounced around the table, although it's generous of him to offer it. Not at all, he said.

The teabag is not his; someone left it at the table because they were running for a train because people never stop run-ning these days. He's making semi-normal sounds. He can hear these sounds and he can hear her tutting agreement. She is not short, the nun. She is ample-sized and wearing silver glasses. She has a bowling-ball bag in green and now she's reading material. Martin John would like to ask her to share this material, but he knows she will not share.

⋯➤

They keep asking him what his name is.

He does not tell them.

Ask him. Ask him. Ask him is all he'll say. He knows. Him who you are all protecting.

When they ask who is he? Who is it that they are all protecting?

He laughs at them and says he is never coming up from the train wheels.

⋯➤

They continue to negotiate.

He wants unfettered access to Euston Station.

They offer him the pork dripping of *come up here* and *we'll talk about it.*

But Martin John is on to them. Come up here until we cuff you.

⋯→

Martin John is still down here beside the wheels of this train. It's cramped, metal-smelly, and he will not rise up to their clamps. They probably have one that will go around his neck, one that they can use to lead him out of this station, like a dog or an unruly horse, into the back of a police van. He's surprised they have not yet come down to collect him.

They move the other train. There's a woman now talking to him. She has lain down on the platform. He can only hear her voice. He will not look at her, even though she has asked him to.

"How are you feeling?"
"It doesn't look very comfortable down there."
"Did you have any breakfast?"
 She does not mention Baldy Conscience.

⋯➔

"I've heard you like the station. We could take a walk together around the station."

She talks about Annie. The announcer. She says she likes Annie's voice better than Jennifer's. Martin John hasn't ever heard Jennifer's voice.

"Are you feeling bad about anything?"

He knows she's lying.

He knows they have the young girl waiting to identify him behind that train.

He knows there's no Jennifer.

She doesn't mention Baldy Conscience.

⋯➔

Martin John has made mistakes.

He's feeling bad about a couple of things all right. He hasn't read the paper today. And he knows they are coming for him. And he knows he cannot stop it. Stop doing *it*.

"Can you move your fingers?"

"Can you show me your hand?"

"Are you hurt?"

He raises one arm.

"We have ambulance men here to help you."

Martin John does not like ambulance men.

He does not respond to her again.

-->

Outside on the station concourse Annie the announcer is telling the hundreds of delayed passengers that *due to an incident, delays are expected at this time and certain trains will not be departing.*

A man in a white shirt with his sleeves rolled up says Oh for fuck's sake. Several others defeat-drift to misery-gate the food court. They buy food they would not have otherwise eaten. Approximately twenty-five exit to smoke. Word moves around the station that there's a man barricaded himself down by the train. The Holyhead train. All sorts of descriptions fly. He's barmy, wearing a hat, he has a weapon, he's barmy, wearing a hat, he might already be dead or electrocuted. He's barmy and he's wearing a hat. They are trying to get his body out now. The NHS is failing mental cases. Thatcher is responsible. If they'd never shut down the asylums . . . You don't know who is going to randomly stab you these days. A woman wearing a camel-coloured coat knew a woman who killed a man because she thought he was Satan. Or maybe that wasn't it. Maybe she killed him because he'd been violently abusing her for years. Which case? That case and this case and the other case all add up to train delays and lock them up or lock them in. One fella says just run him over if he's stupid enough to lie down. In China they'd run him over is another floating point of view. I wish I had the time to throw myself in front of a train, another exhales. And there's the one quiet person always who pretends not to hear or notice because that's the person whose uncle went into the river when the quiet person was fourteen. It's a pretty sad day when someone goes to the line, takes the line to his problems, takes his problems to the wheels of a train. A cousin, a brother of a friend, a young woman—I didn't know her, my friend knew her—all threw themselves in front of trains. Jumpers, they call them jumpers. Is he a jumper? I'm not being rude but I wish he'd chosen another train. Why is it always one that has a boat to meet?

People will be waiting at the other end. How to get word to them? How long is this going to take? We're doing our best, Madam. Sir, I don't know. No you cannot go through the barrier. Wait for an announcement. Watch the board. Stand back. No, you cannot talk to the police. No one's allowed down there. Is he armed? We don't know, we just know you can't board the train.

One man is really, really angry. He swears. He says he's going home to bury his father and if this fucker doesn't get himself out of there he'll personally go down there and kill him and bury the pair of them together. Another joins in and suggests it could be settled if the train rode over him. He's on his way to a music festival and there's a girl involved and he's sorry, he's not being funny like, but if a guy is determined to kill himself this isn't the way to do it, so this guy's obviously a faker and all they got to do is start the train and he'll hop up on the platform and that'll be it. Over. They can all carry on.

There's a bang. People turn. It's just a woman struggling with a suitcase that slipped out of her hand as she tugged it. Sorry, she says, lifting her shoulders a bit for emphasis. It turned on its wheel. The angry brigade budge back from the gate to keep one eye on the board, but not far enough back to admit defeat. It's like they are half-watching a football match while cooking the dinner. They want movement. They're primed, the angry brigade, because most members of the angry-when-the-train-is-late brigade haven't contemplated throwing themselves under or onto the tracks. They just want to get on the fucking train, which is the right of every man or woman who ever thought about getting on a train. Trains for riding, beds for lying in.

Late to the scene: the pelters. Those who are running at full pelt, who know if they aren't already on this train, which they aren't, it is probably gone or about to go so they just push and shovel through the crowd. The ticket inspector hears them approach and moves forward to instruct them to stop, except they think he's generously moving up to scan their ticket and assist them on the fly. Stop, he says. No, you can't go through, there's a delay. There's a problem with a passenger. They only stop when he says emphatically there's a passenger on the line and if you go through there you will die, I mean *he* will die.

Nobody likes being told they'll die. It's a human brake moment. No matter how pumped, how primed, how indignant you are, if you are told even by mistake you could die . . . well even John Smith pauses a moment.

⇢

Ambulance men stand bored. One has bought a fizzy drink, looks like Iron Bru. Another is eating a doughnut. Procedure demands nothing will move until procedure ascertains it can move. Nobody can do anything until procedure has its demands met. Procedure demands that nothing be done until procedure exaggerates its demands. What are procedure's demands? Procedure doesn't know, but there are protocols. They are being followed and thus nothing is happening. The plain people are unhappy.

The woman who left the crowd declaring she was going to stop this is back. She has bought three bottles of Lucozade or possibly more since she has two under one armpit. Excuse me she says to a man in front of her. She aims one of the glass bottles at Martin John's head and fires it onto the track. It misses.

"Why did you do that?"

284

"I want him to move his arm," she says. "I think he's holding something in his hand. He could be armed. I want him to move. I want him out of there."

She puts two bottles into her pocket and shuffles her alignment. She is squinting and concentrating hard.

"If they're not going to move him, I'll move him," she rasps. She lifts another bottle of Lucozade up and hurls it even harder. It hits the side of the train, smashes to clinking glass, liquid, and draws the attention of the procedurals. They move in and remove the Lucozade-throwing woman, who attempts to chuck two bottles at the same time, one of which lands on her own foot.

"He moved, he's moving," some voices say.

Martin John is not moving.

⋯⋙

Martin John has issued his demands.

He says he will not come up from the train wheels unless the entire station is emptied so he can do his circuits alone.

⋯⋙

"What about your job? They will be wondering where you are."

He likes that she imagines he has a job and that a job is waiting on him. That he is useful and people are waiting on him to be useful.

Is there anyone whom it might help him to talk to?

Maybe when he sees the phone, he'll know whom to ring?

Is there someone she should phone in his house?

Martin John does not like the words home and telephone.

Now she has mentioned Baldy Conscience.

Baldy Conscience is in the station.

⇢

Snipers in the roof. Armed and waiting.

They probably have the girl out there too.

Waiting to identify him.

To say he is the one.

Who did the thing.

None of them liked.

But not 'til they noticed it.

And threw the tea.

This will be a problem.

They didn't notice. They never notice and when they do they do not move and he has liked this about *it* before. That no one moves on him. That he can always be assured of the human capacity to be passive.

⇢

There are a few problems down here. He is whispering now because if they know there are problems down here . . . well. And another thing, the smell down here is not good. Nor the cold. Nor the metal. He has positioned himself so his legs are threaded behind two wheels. If the train moves it will cut his legs off. The hospital gown is caught on something. Things are digging into various parts of his body and he has his face towards the undercarriage. His wrist has gone so numb he can't imagine it will work again. The stones that line the railway tracks are embedding themselves absolutely, with some finality, into his flesh. Agony. It's the kind of pain that's poking euphoric. Martin John has tunnelled beyond uncomfortable. But the best thing is his bladder is fuller than even he ever imagined it could be. This, he likes.

Martin John is happy for the entire train service to grind to a halt.

He cannot go up. If he goes up, she will be waiting and it will be over.

Over for you, Martin John, he can hear mam saying.
Can't save you now.

⟶

Big boyos likely bouncing around the station with plans to topple him. The whole of Euston's full of policemen on horses waiting to greet him. Would they form a circle while he walked his circuits? Horse nostrils can be disconcerting. He remembers the smell of wet straw and piddle at Hyde Park.

⟶

Snipers in the roof are already in place. They are possibly trained on the back of his head.

He regrets choosing to face the ground rather than the roof.

Would they also kill the horses to get at him?

⟶

WHAT THEY DON'T KNOW:

Noanie could fix him.

He hadn't even the good grace to come home directly. No, mam had to go over to England and collect him. But first she had to get him outta there. For wasn't he inside again and this time with the Irish sea between them. He'd not just gotten himself in, he'd gotten himself stuffed so far inside she had to plead with them and makes promises to them so they'd let him out. She'd make her life only about him. She would. Oh she would. (When had her life *not* been about him?) It took weeks to convince them. He's very ill, they said. Mentally ill. He's not, she thought. He's just a very bad listener. And she told the doctors this. And they were also very bad listeners.

The single good listener is Noanie, who agrees with her. She'll take her lead from Noanie and him above. When they gave her all kinds of names and titles and explanations she gave them back the bald facts as they stood between her and the file folder notes and those white coats. I've told him. I've warned him for years. I said I was sure. If only he'd heed me but he won't and now he'll pay. They'll kill him if he ends up in there.

In the end she brought Noanie in with her. When Noanie heard the details of what he'd done and how they found him in the station: What? she said. What? Come again? I'm surprised I didn't see that in the paper.

Mam sat beside Noanie and ran through the inventory of warnings she'd given Martin John whilst insisting to the doctors no, no, he's never gone this far, while knowing she had no true idea of how far he might have gone. But he had technically never set a building on fire to her knowledge. A good, hard-working man he is. Was the fire a suicide attempt? I hope so, she thought. I hope so. Please God he'll succeed the next time. She said none of this aloud. Only what she'd learnt to say, I don't know, I don't know and perhaps beneath her breath they might have heard, I don't want to know. Please spare me. Redirect it in the post to someone else.

But they'd an awful thick sheaf of notes on him. They weren't going to let her off easy. They've a big folder on him, she told Noanie on the train back to Hatfield. They do, Noanie said. But he'll get out. They can't afford to keep him in there and they release all the lunatics onto the street and he'll be no different. We'll have him out by the end of the week.

They agreed she could bring him home to Ireland. You'll have to bring him home, Noanie said. 'Til he's stable. Then you can let him come back. Mam didn't want him home. It only seemed like yesterday she'd managed to get rid of him.

He needed a strong hand, mam told the doctors. That was what was missing. A good strong man's hand. Mam offered no explanation as to why a man's hand was missing. Why a man's hand, say, couldn't be found in North or South London. If that was what could fix him? Prison might be the only thing that could fix him. She didn't say it aloud, but she thought it. She thought about what Noanie said. Noanie said lock him in. Lock him in, she said. She didn't say how. The how was her own doing.

He'll have to come home with me. I'll mind him, she said. I'll let him know what's what.

These fellas can do nothing for him, mam told Noanie, who agreed that people who talked in a medical language could do nothing. They can do nothing really, they may as well be talking to the wall for all the sense they make, Noanie said brightly while she fed her green bird. Then she said Timmy the bird would need cleaning out on Thursday and when she cleaned him out she had to let him fly around the room and he'd expect to do his tricks, so if they could get Martin John out of the hospital one way or the other by Thursday it would be for the best. I'll have to clean him, she said, indicating the bottom of his cage. There's only so long he can go without cleaning. Everything has to be right when I clean him or he'll get upset.

⸺➔

They were getting sick of the hospital and the hospital was getting sick of them and Martin John was in-between the lot of them, making no sense at all.

—He's going on about Beirut all the time. It's Beirut this, Beirut that. Why's he doing that, Noanie wanted to know.

—I'll tell you the truth, I think they injected him with something. Or he needs a bang on the head. Or, mam whispered, he's just pretending. Mam swings between two poles. The bash-him and fix-him poles. The sympathy and I'm-sick-of-him poles. The let's end it: It'll-just-take-time poles.

That evening Noanie said brightly they were wasting their time, all of their time, and they needed to put a stop to it. Well Noanie said it as they were eating a trifle that she'd made that day. The only thing I am not satisfied with about this trifle, Noanie said, is the bottom layer. The other two layers I can live with, but there's something missing in the bottom layer. They agreed some mini-oranges or a splash more of sherry might be it.

The rest of the week she and Noanie watched telly together silently.

—It's an awful interruption.

—Oh it is.

—Why couldn't he have paid more heed?

—There was no telling him.

Each evening, with or without trifle, they reached the same conclusion. It was all a waste of their time. All of their time.

—I haven't time to be dealing with this, mam said. I'm not for another minute of it.

She worried though. He'd been away so long and that was a good thing. It was a good thing he'd been away so long as they might not remember when they see him back. Noanie didn't ask what it was they might not remember but they both agreed whomever she didn't want remembering might not remember. Noanie thought she was talking very loosely. No one remembers much anymore, she said. It was no consolation, but mam tried not to think beyond that fact. People forget, do you think? Oh they do, Noanie said, they do.

She had a plan for what she'd do when she got him home. It wasn't a great plan, but it was a plan.

WHAT THEY DIDN'T KNOW:

It would be Mary who got him up in the end.

She works at the French-themed bakery that the majority of passengers trek by to purchase food at the burger and chips joint beside it and her name is Mary and she is devout. Mary and Martin John had once come to blows when he tried to grab hold of her hand as she gave him change for a *pain au chocolat* he didn't really want.

Today Mary is pushing a large rolling rubbish bin down to the massive compactor where the transfer over her head has to be made. It's full of dirty baking paper, napkins and gunk. The compactor, located well out of sight, is beneath the station, for passengers must never be made aware of the volume of disposable muck they create while travelling up/down the country's railways. It requires two people to bring down such an oversize bin, but staff cutbacks have doomed the safe, unobstructed passage of this rolling heap of crap.

There are police officers in her way.
There are random men and women in her way.
There are British Rail people blocking her way.

"You can't go through," an unidentified uniform, appearing from the front of the giant bin, tells her.
    "Well I am not taking this rubbish home to Watford, am I? I work here. I need to bring it down."
    "You'll have to wait. We're not letting anyone through."

Mary is determined she is not taking this crapheap back to the food court because Florence, her Irish supervisor, will only insist Mary return with it again, under the plea *my back, my back love. I can't risk it. It'll put me on a stretcher.*

Mary will wait it out.

It is the mad mesh of all these bodies running into and away from each other, carrying explanations rather than progress, that further frustrate her. Mary is a woman who likes to get things done. Mary is a woman who can get things done. Mary has worked more consecutive hours on this station than some of the light bulbs. She also hasn't eaten for thirty-six hours and is hyper.

A *what's happening?* only gives her: *there's a guy under a train.* A guy under the train is not good, thinks Mary. A guy under the train can mean delays. Is he dead? she asks Anthony, a handsome Nigerian ticket collector with whom she sometimes chit-chats and who is always tired and complaining about his wife, while happily implying Mary could join him anytime for a variety of indulgences. By reply she traditionally provides Romans 10:3, "For they being ignorant of God's righteousness and going about to establish their own righteousness have not submitted themselves unto the righteousness of God," which usually calms his ardour.

Anthony, on this occasion, has more information than Mary.

"No he's not dead. He's not moving, but he's not dead. Stupid guy! Train could have killed him. Trains can kill you. Bam!"

He tells Mary this like she may not have realized trains can kill her. But he is animated. Mary appreciates that he is animated.

Mary, on the verge of sending up an appeal to the Lord, sidles over to have a look. She must ascertain whether there's something going on down there worth burdening the Lord with. She parks the bin out of the way and moves closer so she can neck a peek and see what's going on.

She knows him. Even from this squint she recognizes him. It's the *pain au chocolat* perv. The one she's resorted to discussing scripture with.

"It's him," she thinks. "Damn."

⋯→

"I know him." Mary says loudly. "Let me talk to him. He knows me. I can get him up."

No useless official in charge of the situation believes or trusts Mary, but Mary has long since grown used to being disregarded in both London and by the brotherhood that surrounded her husband in Abuja and now pile into her hallway every Sunday to shout at each other over her. She doesn't listen to them when they crowd out her flat and she won't listen to these clustering spouters who say she can't go down there. Mary is powered by the Lord, not railway officials. So she calls across the waist-high glass which houses the public from the buffers below. She calls out to the back of Martin John's head.

"You! Get up here now and stop being so stupid!"

⋯→

Mary has a good reason to call across to the man on the tracks. He's in her way. He's holding up the trains. He needs to get out of her way. Tonight is Mary's chance. For weeks she's awaited her turn. Several women in her Watford Women's Ministry were ahead of her. There's a roster. She has listened to her sisters. She has nodded at the sisters and delighted in each sister's response to a selected Bible reading while secretly counting down to her moment. A sister's talent for lifting the word of God off the page is not created equally. She may get up on the horse of God but can she hold her saddle? Can she lute his words? Because the simple fact is yawning can set in. She has seen it. She has yawned it and tonight's her night to present her practiced preaching. How she has silently prepared these words while putting a hundred ham-and-cheese croissants inside paper bags for indifferent passengers.

Last night she barely slept, her tongue locomoting its way around the words-upon-words that must accumulate to form her exhortation. She's spent seven weeks waiting to strike at Satan. In spite of the fact that she's merely been asked to talk lightly on a reading of Mark 5:9, she has tasked herself to wholly and vigorously rev up the Watford Women's Ministry. To go beyond the polite sharing of readings, biscuits and the passive desire to repent amid side discussions on waxing and buying a washing machine on tick. There must be more! She wants to inspire! She has fasted in anticipation of more.

Usually no sister stands up. Heads down, they struggle to find the line in the Bible, they mutter apologetically, they mumble out more apologies and eee-nough. Enough! Tonight will be different. It's time to bust out the Lord. She knows where and how her crescendo will land. Boom! She has left nothing to chance. Bust him out! Boom! BUST HIM OUT is where she'll terminate. For dramatic effect her arms will lift to the ceiling, her Bible will drop to the floor. This is her plan. Except this duffer lying on the railway track of Platform 6 is threatening the primary lift-off from that folding chair. Without a launch there can be no landing. Also, she needs to wash her hair. How can she be urging the five other women to bust the Lord out if she's stood with lackluster hair. Lackluster, she rumbles to herself.

Gone, gone, gone, get Satan gone. Satan get gone. Get gone Satan, Satan get gone. Mary pecks out in guttural whispers. Bust him out. First, though, bust him in. The Lord is in touch. This is real. This is it. This is why she slept so lightly last night.

I am open, Mary thinks. *I am open to whatever the Lord sends me.*

Here it is, craven-curled before her. In this surprising location the Lord has sent her a numpty-headed nutter whom she must raise from the rails. It is unfortunate. Inconvenient. But Minister Janice has warned that the Lord strikes in mysterious ways and here he's striking beyond mysterious, here he is boldly challenging Mary to tread the turbulent water, canoe through and defeat the prospect of the 4:12 pm train to Watford Junction being further delayed.

It has been a long shift since 6:30 am. She's been fasting for 36 hours ahead of tonight's meeting. Caged and overheating in the cramped bakery, she is tired of invisible interactions with fleeing passengers, endlessly frustrated by the limits of the human hand. She is irked by Florence, her supervisor, who today potted Mary up at the back, washing baking trays clamped in grease and burn. If Mary is to reach into the hearts of heathens, God's unbelievers, no matter that they are rude, distrustful, dismissive and, not uncommonly, demented, she must be out front, handing over paper bags. Her plan to inscribe biblical quotes on a stack of them during her first tea break had been punctured by Florence informing her that, because they were a person short on the late shift, there will be no breaks, unless Mary wants to work the double shift. We have to get ahead, said Florence after Mary had told her no, no way, not as long as there was air in her lungs can she work a double shift today because tonight she has an important event.

"What's that then?" smirked Florence, "you rushing off to get married or something?"

Florence is an unbeliever. Florence doesn't have Jesus in her heart. Mary's compassion that Florence could one day be saved diminishes the longer she has to share this kennel of a bake house and endure Florence's unrepentant digs at her faith. There are only three topics she can discuss with Florence and one of them is Debenhams. The other is Flo's grandkids and the third The Menopause. Flo uses the latter to argue she can't stand too close to the oven or she'll melt. To prove her point Flo once faux-fainted and Mary had the brilliant idea to kick her in the kidney to find out if she really was a-faint. The kick brought a howl: Why'd you do that? I thought you were dead, said Mary. I wanted to wake you up. Her slick response further solidified Mary's faith because she had never been this quick in the past. Florence takes her supervisory role very seriously when it comes to ordering Mary to take the giant rubbish bin down and empty it. No disrespect, she'll say. I went to Catholic school and it was shit and I've had it up to here with the Pope, can you take the rubbish down for me, love? My back's bad and you've got Jesus on your side.

⸺➤

"You," she called.

"You," she called again at the distant pale green bundle below.

"You," she shouted.

Nobody heard Mary.

Nobody saw Mary.

Mary saw Martin John.

Him. She told herself. Him. Again. She knew he'd come again. She'd warned him that time he'd grabbed her hand if he ever did it again she'd cut it off him. But he'd come back often and they'd talked about the Bible and she felt he was making progress.

The train standing at Platform 5 is the delayed . . .

The train standing at Platform 9 is the train for Crewe. Always keep your luggage to yourself. Unattended baggage will be removed and destroyed.

Trains are backing up. Mary does not like the *train at platform is the delayed . . .* People drift. Stop to look. Cops cop on. A white man with a skinny, misshapen head is moving into position with his loudhailer. Some white men have the weirdest heads, thinks Mary watching him.

"Please move away from the area," Head intones. The more he *please move aways,* the more people come closer and escape around him, determined to get into the train, determined that the train will depart because they have somewhere to go, no matter there's a man wedged underneath it.

⋯→

"What happened?"

"How'd he get down there?"

"Did he jump? He must have jumped."

"Did he go out the wrong door?"

"Probably a pissed-off train driver."

"What happened?"

"Is he pissed?

"No, he's mad."

"He's not mad. He's lonely."

"Crap. He's not lonely. He's mad."

"Everyone's mad these days."

"Some are madder than others."

"What's going on?"

"Oh my God!" A woman says. "Look, his gown is open. Eww. His bum. That's *disgusting.*"

"Cover him up."

"They should cover him up, that's not right."

This shifts a few people away. A third woman paddles off stating to no one in particular that this has got to stop. Whatever is up with these people has got to be stopped and Irish bombers cause it all. She's going to stop it. At the word terrorist, the other two women abruptly depart.

⋯→

"I know him," Mary says.

"Who is he?"

"Just a guy. Hangs around inside where I work. He's harmless."

A policeman loudhails in her right ear.

302

MOVE PLEASE. EVERYONE MOVE. WE NEED
YOU TO CLEAR THE AREA.

"I work here," says Mary. "I'm not moving. I know him."
She knows him, the passengers endorse.

"I know how to get him up. I can get him up. He'll
listen to me."

⋯→

No one accepts that Mary can levitate Martin John the way
no one accepted Jesus could heal the sick. No one accepts
the Lord because they have not found the Lord. Mary has.
Mary knows. Mary, wearing her apron, will galvanize this
crowd of lugs to repentance. It's bigger than a prayer meeting. Any prayer meeting. Anywhere. Ever. Jesus has called
her at Euston.

Utters a curse does Mary. Acts like she intends to move
back and comply. Retreats to the giant parked bin. Mary
has had enough. They are in her way and her train home is
threatened. For each time she has not been seen, for every
rude and disgraceful customer, for every extra minute spent
not being compensated, for every evaluation endured by
that annoying supervisor and for the hundreds of times
she has struggled with this intractable, smelly bin—Mary
has had it.

She observes the backs of the police muttering, mith-
ering and moving matters no place. She pushes past them
with the rubbish bin ahead of her.

HEY!

STOP!

Mary protests, while pushing deftly on, that she works
in the station and is just doing her job.

Mary walks steadily. She lifts the handles of this impossible wheeled skip up above her shoulders. She about-turns
the contraption, checks left and right for people in her path
and parks the bin near the top of Platform 4, where the

reformed croissant perv is crunched below on the rails opposite. For now there is no train between them. Down she kneels by the platform edge, camouflaged by the giant bin.

"You!" she says. "It's me Mary. Mary from inside."

He bunches his body up further.

A slight roll away from her, he folds his arm in and puts his hand between his legs.

"You know. Me from the bakery."

She has some idea about negotiation. She heard an interview on the radio with Terry Waite seven years ago. "Cast off Satan and get up here now," she whispers. The bundle moves. He may be moving. Is he going to look at her? This has prospects if she's rapid.

"Look, whatever sin took you down there, let it bring you right back up! Come on. *Rise!*"

Rise curls him up noticeably tighter. He pulls his knees up. Stay calm, thinks Mary. Let him know there's help.

"Talking can help. At least talk to me . . ."

Alleviate hopelessness, thinks Mary.

"Everyone feels like shit. It's Monday. It's pissing rain. We're all miserable. Come back up and be miserable." He has not spoken. But he also has not moved. This is better.

"Fasting can help. I've been fasting. Devil gets nervous when you're fasting. He can't reach you if you're not full of food. . . . 'And Jesus asked . . . what is thy name? And he said Legion: because many devils were entered into him.' **Luke, 8:30**, remember?"

"We're all sinners. Devil's on the loose. You're just the biggest sinner right now in this station. But in five minutes there'll be another sinner. It's what he does. He hops, he spreads, he congeals. So release him. Bust him out! Let others take the burden. Do not hold him in. Share!"

Behind her, the wheels of an arriving train make tightening, ever tightening, whuh whuh vrrrar va-vrrar sounds. Sounds that close in on her, metal-on-metal registering in the roots of her teeth, a screech that forces her to raise her voice. Passengers will descend. Passengers will see her down here. Passengers could sink her progress.

"You think you've gone too far, right? You think it's all impossible. But you haven't gone far enough. That's the problem."

At this, his body, unfortunately, shifts to join his bunched-up legs. He's gone. Completely obscured under the train. Damn. She can't see him. Damn. They'll blame her. Damn. Damn. Damn. Behind her, train doors open. Passengers descend. Passengers are looking at her queer, down on her knees pleading with the bottom stripe of paint on the train opposite. The sudden spread of passengers conceals her though, offering vital negotiation time. Police are flooded: she can hear them diverting, directing, declaring.

"Don't make me come down there."

"DUE TO AN UNFORESEEN INCIDENT WE ARE EXPERIENCING DELAYS. UPDATES WILL BE POSTED ON THE BOARD."

"That's it. Up here now or I am coming down to get you up."

"DUE TO AN UNFORESEEN INCIDENT WE ARE EXPERIENCING DELAYS. UPDATES WILL BE POSTED ON THE BOARD."

"Oh for fuck's sake. Get up here now."

"DUE TO AN UNFORESEEN INCIDENT WE ARE EXPERIENCING DELAYS. UPDATES WILL BE POSTED ON THE BOARD."

If I miss my fucking train because of him . . . she thinks. The combination of fury and hunger push Mary further to the platform edge, but she cannot see a thread of him. Down she lies to squint. Where is he? The concrete presses on her breastbone and squashes her mammaries. If she could just see how far under the train he has gone. Maybe poke him decisively. Grab him by the arm. Then he'd move. She's getting ideas. The Lord is giving them to her. She's never been this motivated to deliver salvation unto another before. He needs disturbing. She can disturb him. She has mere seconds before they rumble her. Mary slides down the wall a little bit, the way you might dip your foot undecided into a swimming pool then retrieve it. Part way down, she changes her mind and tries to tricep back up, but her hand slips, which lurches her forward, feet stutter-shock onto the strange pick-axed-apart-looking stones. A left-inclined tumble to crunch, ouch, fuck as she planks onto the side of her left hip, elbow smacking off a rail. Ow! What in the shitting hell of mercy is she doing down here? This was a very bad idea. How's she going to get back up? No way she's going over there. She immediately strikes to clamber back up onto the platform, but her too-tight pencil skirt impedes her. Left knee scrapes ugly against the wall. Very pissed off, she turns, squats, to emit a final yell.

JUST COME OUT HERE RIGHT NOW.

He turns his head a touch. He can definitely hear her.

"I'm fucking stuck. Help me right now you moron. I have a child. They'll arrest me. Quick. I swear they're coming. Fuck. You've got to help me." She has lost Jesus down here, she has found only a tirade of F-words and the desire to see this man extinguished and herself airlifted to glory.

Something's moving under there. She can hear the stones shuffle.

┄➔

The worst part of it, from Mary's point of view, is that the policeman with the misshapen head is now heaving under one of her armpits to get her back on the platform. It's been a long, sweaty shift and she does not want this particular man in her armpit. *I've got her, I've got her, legs, someone grab the legs. Someone get her other leg. Push.* Two others are clawing at her other armpit and there's another jumped down to the track and his hand is pushing up her bum, which is pure unnecessary chancery. Shameful, she

306

would later say aloud. One voice remarks on how heavy she is, as some kind of reassurance they are all doing a great job. Her knee scrapes along the platform edge as the punishing thought an Intercity 125 train might arrive from Manchester any second and crush her. She doesn't care if Martin John lives or dies at this point. She doesn't care about tonight's meeting. She just wants back up and out of this swollen volume of manhandling.

On the way back up the platform, pain revisits her palms from pressing on the concrete and there's a slicing sting beneath her tights from the knee gash. Head lectures onward and upward in undulating clips about the danger of doing such a stupid thing and how she needs to listen when police tell her what to do and they may yet arrest her for obstruction.

"Obviously I didn't want to go down there, it was an accident," she says. "I slipped. Innit."

The better part is it takes two police officers to move the bin along behind her. At the top of the platform while they are asking Mary how to spell her name and writing it into three different notebooks, Martin John is led away by a group of people near her. He is barefoot. His gown is open at the back. His hand reaches behind to hold it closed in some desperate stab at a dignity he'd long lost.

"THAT is the saddest thing," she declares to Anthony nearby, ignoring her as he fiddles with a button on the side of his digital watch. "Totally unnecessary. Never need happen. People are so isolated. That's why they should go to church."

"What's the date today?" Anthony, still jamming at his watch.

24-HOUR CCTV RECORDING IS IN OPERATION AT THIS STATION FOR THE PURPOSE OF SECURITY AND SAFETY MANAGEMENT.

"I told you I could get him up," Mary says to no one in particular. "I got him up," she says triumphantly as she trundles off with the bin.

WHAT THEY DON'T KNOW:

Before he went to the railway tracks.

Martin John has left the food court. He flew it hurrying. He more than flew it hurrying. He is in bolt. No one, except him, is quite sure why this half-dressed man has taken up such speed.

A situation, a situation is boiling/bubbling, a situation that must be burst. He must circle it. If he can circuit the station, the situation will be circled. Harm was done, harm was done, so the loop gnaws. Did he or did he not just grab her? Did he lift his gown? He did lift his gown. His hands were under it.

The nun put Martin John in a bad way. This is the refrain he'll give us. A circuit. A circuit. Only a circuit will erase it. He is barefoot. He is green-gowned. But a circuit, an absolute circuit, which will need to be a square circuit because the station is a box.

He did not touch the nun. He knows he did not touch the nun. Harm was done. He is covered in tea. His arm is wet. His shoulder is wet because Harm was done.

⋯➔

Martin John has told us about the nun, but she never was the sole captive of his attention. He has lied to us about this. He has lied to us about much. Has he lied to us about Baldy Conscience?

Her, over there, sat next to her parents, she's the reason he sat down here. The nun may be here too. That's her choice. But Martin John's choice was towards the young one with long brown hair. She lifts a burger up and down to her mouth. Her eyes do not initially notice him. He diddles about with the tea, but his hand has slipped/passed under the table over his groin. At first he applies pressure from the heel of his palm to his general bulge but as her mouth moves and munches, his subtle mounding movements become strong, flat-palmed, insistent. Up and down. Until he resists no more and macerates it. He's waiting for her to register him. He's patient, though. Her hair shades her face and she's concentrating on her burger. He watches her lips and how she wipes them with the back of her hand mid-sentence. He likes it. She's somewhere around fifteen or so. Maybe more. Maybe less. Maybe he doesn't know. Maybe he doesn't care. Her head moves between her food and the conversation to her left. Martin John's hand below remains firmly with her and he likes what she's doing for him. He's lost (in)to it now. He doesn't notice the man who has joined him at the table to his left because his right hand has found its way under his gown and his legs have parted and he's leaning backwards and focused hard on his task.

⋯→

People do what people do. They wonder. They elbow. They lean and whisper. They nod. They query. Do you think? Is he? Each other. Doing that? They stand up and look about for someone to report it to. They look for someone to report it to using their arms. They might even walk towards someone panicked and point. They may wave a hand and indicate the problem. Excuse me there's a guy over here who . . . or they may just up and move away from what's happening and allow that someone else will deal with it. Very occasionally there's a decisive someone who sees it. They have seen it and they know exactly what it is they are seeing.

⋯→

Not today though. Not today.

⋯→

Or maybe. Wait now.

⋯→

Hold on a second.

⋯→

It's the man at the next table who, like others, thought he saw what he saw, except, ever-assured, never feels the need to question what he sees, knows it's what he saw and requires no further confirmation of what he saw. He does not ever move off and find another table when he's uncomfortable. He stays here. He believes in conclusive ends. He likes them.

⋯→

Martin John's tea has been forgotten.
Except by the man at the next table.
Martin John is being watched.
Carefully watched.
Measured.

⋯→

The man at the next table sits back. His hands go into his pockets.

⋯→

They've seen each other at it before. In this station. They exchange knowing glances. One has watched the other up to it. The other has watched the one up to it. Two men up to it. They have never spoken. But one has followed the other. One has sometimes watched the other from a bench. The other has encouraged being observed. Sometimes afterwards the one, Martin John, will look at the other and the other will know he's being watched. *Score* says the look. He likes being watched. Once Martin John went after the same woman after the other had managed it.

Years now.
They've been silent pairs.
Sometimes it's singles. Sometimes it's doubles.

⋯→

That's how he met Ralph. That's how he came to live in Ralph's house. Did each other a favour. Except Ralph went too far, very far. He went indoors with it. Martin John wouldn't do what Ralph did but he didn't mind looking at the photos Ralph took of it.

⋯→

Did he grab her? Did he lift his gown? Did she or did she not just leap back from him? Might have been a young one. Not a woman exactly. Girl. Tall girl. Teen girl. He is confused. Wrong to touch a girl. Had he gone for a girl before? He had. Harm was done. He grabbed her. It was fast. Aggressive. He lunged. He is covered in tea along one arm and on his shoulder. She covered him in tea or someone near her covered him in tea. But if it was she, then not a girl. Girl doesn't have tea. Woman has tea. Father has tea.

Past John Menzies in corner, cold air baptizing his flesh through gown. Wristband inscribed with his name and nothing to hide it. He covers it with the palm of his other hand, pressing hard.

All is wrong. Sixth busiest train station. Too many people. Not enough people. Away from the light. Backward. Lifters coming. Bumps into woman. Pile of bags. Platform 1. Not Platform 18. Big interruptions. Circuit will not start. Ever. Retreats to seat. Person stands. Removes. Word has travelled. They are clearing the way.

Start this before all is ended by whole lot here who want *it* stopped, the way he wants it stopped. No, not it. He doesn't want the circuit stopped. He wants it whole. Just once. He wants the other stopped. Maybe. Maybe he does and maybe he doesn't.

He bangs into the wrong man to bang into on this day in this station. Banged-into-man shoves him off his legs. Smacked, down he goes onto his shoulder, which is tea-wet. Bald man with Millwall face leering over him now, *if* and *he* and *fucking* and *ever* and he boots Martin John a strong kick. Three more. Martin John covers his wristband. He doesn't want anyone to read it. That is it. All he has. Others come. Heads are shaking.

⇢

Phones will happen. Police. Rain will fall. Overhead Annie. Numbers. Stations. All she has ever said gone. Wiped. Circuit is gone. Wiped. All is gone. All is gone Martin John.

All is gone except where he's going. Barriers, but those sloppy ticket men take off for chats. Don't look up from their newspapers. *Keep the head down, Martin John*, said mam. Head can pass. Minutes will end. Just minutes. Mere minute. Martin John holds his wristband and will on.

WHAT THEY DON'T KNOW:

In the Chair.

Mam tied his two wrists to the arms of the Chair. He didn't struggle, just sat there limp, slouched like he'd been stuffed.

⋯➤

The mornings were the worst. He was shaky in the mornings. He was strange until he took the tablets. He shook a little less, but slouched more. It was like someone had unpacked his innards and repacked them tighter, yet still tangled.

⋯➤

He didn't seem to know where he was. It was for the best, she thought.
She was unable to think beyond it is for the best.

⋯➤

All for the best, everything for the best, if he's gone it's for the best, if he's back it's for the best, if it goes away it's for the best, best not to dwell on it, best not to dwell on what he did or didn't do or couldn't do or might do or would do. Best also not to dwell on should. What should she do? Not dwell on it. For the best, no dwelling. He could dwell though. He could dwell in the Chair. For the best. Where she'd know exactly where he was. Best. Indeed, very best.

⋯➤

I did what I did and I stand by what I did. What would you do?

⋯➤

Mam wanted her, the girl, to know that she had him tied safely into the Chair. I thought she'd feel better. That was why I told her he was back. I said he's in a very bad way and to be honest, she didn't look sympathetic. She hurried away from me. She looked afraid. I was going to follow her, but I didn't follow her.

⋯→

He is back in his chair.
In the Chair not so much can go wrong. She puts the telly on for him.
In the Chair he gets tea. That's how it is in the Chair.

⋯→

Everything I done was to keep Martin John on the outside.
You understand.
To keep him out.
Now he's inside.
We're done in.

The P List.

Pre-election, power-sharing, pointed, prescribing, psychiatrist, potent, partly, plummets, price, petrol, peg, partner, people, pipes, political, parliament, publicly, pay, pretty, products, performance, poorest, perilous, paints, pay, parliament, periodically, poisoning, prison, promoted, people, put, part, part, prepared, parliament, purse, peoples, pink, paid, portray, paving, pre-boomtown.

Possible, Paisley, political, politician, political, politicians, people, part, pay, parliament, pointed, pills, patent, potent, pain, plummet.

People, position, proposal, position, prominent, provide, piling, part, prospect, present, private, profit, pains, partner, profit, part, Voltaire.

—Would you do the Bs for me there, Martin John, good lad?

It was a time when people didn't ask as many questions. That was the time it was.

⋯➔

It is never defined.

Acknowledgements

I gratefully acknowledge the financial support of the Canada Council for the Arts and the British Columbia Arts Council. I heartily thank the many writers' festivals, libraries, colleges and communities that invited me to read.

Thank you Dr. Paul Fedoroff for referring me to *Psychopathia Sexualis* and for sending me a fascinating chapter of his own work. My thanks also to Dr. Alex Langford for answering questions on the NHS & Dr. Jenny Svanberg, Dr. Barry Segal and Nancy Smith for their help.

Thank you for patience, precision, and collaboration to my editor John Metcalf, my pure decent publisher Dan Wells, and my holy miracle of a copy editor Emily Donaldson and my agent Marilyn Biderman. I am grateful to Grant, Kate, Chris and Andrew at Biblioasis for all their hard work.

Merci mille fois Marie-Lulu pour tes encouragements incessants, ta brillante intelligence et ta lecture sans fin. Thank you Tamara Faith Berger, Daniel Allen Cox for gritty exchange, Juliane Okot Bitek for reading Mary and endless Acholi laughter, Daniel Handler for excellent dispatches on reading, Marina Roy for French/English literary/art discourse and Arabella & Lindsay for author photo and wine.

Go raibh míle maith agaibh for the decades of love, support and laughter to Niamh Barrett, Edel Ni Chonchubhair, Cathy Dillon, Mary McCarthy in Dublin, Siobhán, Ita, Tara (ah here, AK), Carol in Vancouver and for recent good times and Quakers in New York, Helen Graves & Ann Kjellberg.

Much love to my son Cúán Isamu, the most voracious reader, chip eater and funniest fella I know. Mo Cheol Thú!

Anakana Schofield won the Amazon.ca First Novel Award and the Debut-Litzer Prize for Fiction in 2013 for her debut novel *Malarky*. *Malarky* was also nominated for the Ethel Wilson Fiction Prize, selected as a Barnes & Noble Discover Great New Writers pick and named on many Best Book of the Year lists for 2012 and 2013. *Martin John*, her critically acclaimed second novel, was shortlisted for the Giller Prize. Schofield contributes criticism and essays to the *London Review of Books* blog, *The Guardian*, *The Irish Times*, the *Globe and Mail* and more.

Dear readers,

We rely on subscriptions from people like you to tell these other stories – the types of stories most publishers consider too risky to take on.

Our subscribers don't just make the books physically happen. They also help us approach booksellers, because we can demonstrate that our books already have readers and fans. And they give us the security to publish in line with our values, which are collaborative, imaginative and 'shamelessly literary'.

All of our subscribers:

- receive a first-edition copy of each of the books they subscribe to
- are thanked by name at the end of these books
- are warmly invited to contribute to our plans and choice of future books

BECOME A SUBSCRIBER, OR GIVE A SUBSCRIPTION TO A FRIEND

Visit andotherstories.org/subscribe to become part of an alternative approach to publishing.

Subscriptions are:

£20 for two books per year

£35 for four books per year

£50 for six books per year

OTHER WAYS TO GET INVOLVED

If you'd like to know about upcoming events and reading groups (our foreign-language reading groups help us choose books to publish, for example) you can:

- join the mailing list at: andotherstories.org/join-us
- follow us on Twitter: @andothertweets
- join us on Facebook: facebook.com/AndOtherStoriesBooks
- follow our blog: Ampersand

This book was made possible thanks to the support of:

Aaron McEnery · Abigail Dawson · Abigail Miller · Ada Gokay · Adam Lenson · Adriana Maldonado · Aileen-Elizabeth Taylor · Aino Efraimsson · Ajay Sharma · Alan Ramsey · Alasdair Hutchison · Alasdair Thomson · Alastair Dickson · Alastair Gillespie · Alastair Maude · Alec Begley · Alex Gregory · Alex Martin · Alex Ramsey · Alex Robertson · Alex Sutcliffe · Alexander Balk · Alexandra Buchler · Alexandra Citron · Alexandra de Scitivaux · Alexandra Georgescu · Ali Conway · Ali Smith · Alice Brett · Alison Hughes · Alison Layland · Allison Graham · Allyson Dowling · Alyse Ceirante · Amanda · Amanda Dalton · Amanda DeMarco · Amelia Ashton · Amelia Dowe · Amy Allebone-Salt · Amy McDonnell · Amy Rushton · Anderson Tepper · Andrew Kerr-Jarrett · Andrew Marston · Andrew McCafferty · Andrew Rego · Andy Chick · Andy Madeley · Angela Creed · Angela Everitt · Angus MacDonald · Ann Van Dyck · Anna Holmwood · Anna Milsom · Anna Solovyev · Anna Vinegrad · Anna-Maria Aurich · Annalise Pippard · Anne Carus · Anne Meadows · Anne Stokes · Anne Marie Jackson · Anonymous · Anonymous · Anonymous · Anthony Carrick · Anthony Quinn · Antonia Lloyd-Jones · Antonio de Swift · Antony Pearce · Aoife Boyd · Aoife McCarthy · Archie Davies · Asako Serizawa · Asher Norris · Audrey Mash · Averill Buchanan · Avril Joy · Barbara Adair · Barbara Anderson · Barbara Devlin · Barbara Mellor · Barbara Robinson · Barry Hall · Barry John Fletcher · Bartolomiej Tyszka · Belinda Farrell · Ben Paynter · Ben Schofield · Ben Smith · Ben Thornton · Benjamin Judge · Benjamin Morris · Bernard Devaney · Beth Mcintosh · Bianca Jackson · Bianca Winter · Bill Myers · Blanka Stoltz · Bob Hill · Bob Richmond-Watson · Briallen Hopper · Brigita Ptackova · C Mieville · Cam Scott · Candy

Says Juju Sophie · Carl Emery · Carla Coppola · Carol Mavor · Carol McKay · Caroline Maldonado · Caroline Perry · Caroline Smith · Catherine Taylor · Catrin Ashton · Cecilia Rossi and Iain Robinson · Cecily Maude · Charles Lambert · Charles Rowley · Charlotte Holtam · Charlotte Middleton · Charlotte Ryland · Charlotte Whittle · Charlotte Murrie & Stephen Charles · Chris Day · Chris Fawson · Chris Gribble · Chris Holmes · Chris Lintott · Chris Stevenson · Chris Vardy · Chris Watson · Chris Wood · Chris Elcock · Christine Carlisle · Christine Luker · Christopher Allen · Christopher Jackson · Christopher Terry · Ciara Ní Riain · Claire Brooksby · Claire Fuller · Claire Trevien · Claire Williams · Claire C Riley · Clare Quinlan · Clarissa Botsford · Clemence Sebag · Clifford Posner · Clive Bellingham · Clodie Vasli · Colette Dunne · Colin Burrow · Colin Matthews · Courtney Lilly · Dan Pope · Daniel Arnold · Daniel Carpenter · Daniel Coxon · Daniel Gallimore · Daniel Gillespie · Daniel Hahn · Daniel Hugill · Daniel Lipscombe · Daniela Steierberg · Dave Lander · Davi Rocha · David Hebblethwaite · David Hedges · David Higgins · David Johnson-Davies · David Roberts · David Shriver · David Smith · Dawn Hart · Debbie Pinfold · Deborah Bygrave · Deborah Jacob · Denis Stillewagt and Anca Fronescu · Dermot McAleese · Dianna Campbell · Dimitris Melicertes · Dominique Brocard · Duncan Marks · Duncan Ranslem · Ed Tallent · Elaine Rassaby · Eleanor Maier · Eleanor Walsh · Elisabeth Jaquette · Eliza O'Toole · Elizabeth Cochrane · Elizabeth Heighway · Ellen Jones · Elsbeth Julie Watering · Emily Diamand · Emily Gray · Emily Jeremiah · Emily Taylor · Emily Yaewon Lee & Gregory Limpens · Emma Bielecki · Emma Perry · Emma Teale · Emma Timpany · Emma Yearwood · Emma Louise

Grove · Eva Tobler-Zumstein · Ewan Tant · Finbarr Farragher · Fiona Graham · Fiona Quinn · Fran Sanderson · Frances Hazelton · Francesca Caracciolo · Francis Taylor · Friederike Knabe · G Thrower · Gabrielle Crockatt · Gawain Espley · Gemma Tipton · Genevra Richardson · Genia Ogrenchuk · Geoffrey Urland · George McCaig · George Savona · George Wilkinson · George Quentin Baker · George Sandison & Daniela Laterza · Georgia Panteli · Gerard Mehigan · Gill Boag-Munroe · Gillian Spencer · Gillian Stern · Glenys Vaughan · Gordon Cameron · Graham & Steph Parslow · Graham R Foster · Gregory Conti · Guy Haslam · Hannah Perret · Hans Lazda · Harriet Mossop · Heather Fielding · Helen Collins · Helen Poulsen · Helen Brady · Helene Walters-Steinberg · Henriette Heise · Henrike Laehnemann · Henry Hitchings · Ian Barnett · Ian Kirkwood · Ian McMillan · Ian Smith · Ian Stephen · Íde Corley · Ignês Sodré · Inna Carson · Irene Mansfield · Isabella Weibrecht · Isobel Staniland · J Collins · JA Calleja · Jack Brown · Jack McNamara · Jacqueline Taylor · Jacqueline Lademann · Jakob Hammarskjöld · James Beck · James Clark · James Cubbon · James Lee · James Portlock · James Scudamore · James Tierney · James Warner · Jamie Walsh · Jan Vijverberg · Jane Crookes · Jane Whiteley · Jane Woollard · Janet Mullarney · Janette Ryan · Jarred McGinnis · Jasmin Kate Kirkbride · Jasmine Gideon · JC Sutcliffe · Jean-Jacques Regouffre · Jeff Collins · Jeffrey Davies · Jennifer Hearn · Jennifer Higgins · Jennifer Hurstfield · Jennifer O'Brien · Jenny Diski · Jenny Newton · Jeremy Faulk · Jeremy Weinstock · Jerry Simcock · Jess Conway · Jess Howard-Armitage · Jess Parsons · Jessica Kingsley · Jethro Soutar · Jim Boucherat · Jo Harding · Joanna Flower · Joanna Luloff · Joanna Neville · Joel Love · Johan Forsell ·

Johanna Eliasson · Johannes Menzel · John Conway · John Down · John Gent · John Hodgson · John Kelly · John Nicholson · John Royley · John Steigerwald · Jon Riches · Jon Lindsay Miles · Jonathan Evans · Jonathan Ruppin · Jonathan Watkiss · Joseph Cooney · Joseph Schreiber · Joshua Davis · Josie Soutar · JP Sanders · Judith Blair · Julia Thum · Julian Duplain · Julian Lomas · Juliane Jarke · Julie Gibson · Julie Van Pelt · Juliet Swann · Kaarina Hollo · Katarina Trodden · Kate Cooper · Kate Gardner · Kate Griffin · Kate Pullinger · Katharina Liehr · Katharine Freeman · Katharine Robbins · Katherine El-Salahi · Katherine Jacomb · Katherine Skala · Kathryn Bogdanow-itsch-Johnston · Kathryn Edwards · Kathryn Lewis · Katie Brown · Katja Bell · Keith Dunnett · Keith Walker · Kelly Russell · Kent McKernan · Kevin Brockmeier · Kevin Pino · Kevin Winter · Kiera Vaclavik · KL Ee · Kristin Djuve · Krystalli Glyniadakis · Lana Selby · Lander Hawes · Laura Batatota · Laura Clarke · Laura Drew · Lauren Ellemore · Laurence Laluyaux · Leanne Bass · Leeanne O'Neill · Leonie Schwab · Lesley Lawn · Lesley Watters · Leslie Rose · Linda Broadbent · Linda Dalziel · Lindsay Brammer · Lindsey Ford · Linette Bruno · Liz Ketch · Loretta Platts · Lorna Bleach · Louise Bongiovanni · Louise Rogers · Luc Verstraete · Luke Williams · Lynda Graham · Lynn Martin · M Manfre · Mac York · Maeve Lambe · Maggie Humm · Maggie Peel · Maggie Redway · Maisie & Nick Carter · Mandy Boles · Margaret Jull Costa · Margaret E Briggs · Maria Cotera · Marie Bagley · Marie Donnelly · Marina Castledine · Marina Galanti · Marina Jones · Mark Ainsbury · Mark Lumley · Marlene Adkins · Martha Gifford · Martha Nicholson · Martin Brampton · Martin Conneely · Martin Hollywood · Martin Cromie · Mary Nash · Mary Wang · Mathias Enard · Matt & Owen Davies · Matthew Francis · Matthew Geden · Matthew Lawrence · Matthew O'Dwyer · Matthew Smith · Matthew Thomas ·

Maureen McDermott · Maxime Dargaud-Fons · Meaghan Delahunt · Megan Wittling · Melissa Beck · Melissa Quignon-Finch · Melvin Davis · Merima Jahic · Meryl Hicks · Michael Holtmann · Michael Johnston · Michael Moran · Michelle Bailat-Jones · Michelle Roberts · Michelle Dyrness · Milo Waterfield · Miranda Persaud · Miranda Petruska · Monika Olsen · Morgan Lyons · Murali Menon · Najiba · Natalie Brandweiner · Natalie Smith · Nathan Rostron · Nayla Hadchiti · Neil Griffiths · Neil Pretty · Nia Emlyn-Jones · Nick Chapman · Nick Sidwell · Nick James · Nick Nelson & Rachel Eley · Nicola Hart · Nicola Hughes · Nina Alexandersen · Nina Power · Nuala Watt · Octavia Kingsley · Olga Alexandru · Olga Zilberbourg · Olivia Heal · Olivier Pynn · Owen Booth · Pablo Rossello · Pamela Ritchie · Pat Crowe · Pat Morgan · Patricia Appleyard · Patricia McCarthy · Patrick Owen · Paul Bailey · Paul Brand · Paul Gamble · Paul Griffiths · Paul Hannon · Paul Jones · Paul Millar · Paul Munday · Paul Myatt · Paul C Daw · Paul M. Cray · Paula Edwards · Penelope Hewett Brown · Peter Armstrong · Peter Law · Peter McCambridge · Peter Rowland · Peter Vilbig · Peter Vos · Philbert Xavier · Philip Warren · Philippa Wentzel · Phillip Canning · Phyllis Reeve · Piet Van Bockstal · PJ Abbott · Poppy Collinson · PRAH Recordings · Rachael MacFarlane · Rachael Williams · Rachel Carter · Rachel Kennedy · Rachel Lasserson · Rachel Van Riel · Rachel Watkins · Rea Cris · Read MAW Books · Rebecca Atkinson · Rebecca Braun · Rebecca Carter · Rebecca Moss · Rebecca Rosenthal · Réjane Collard-Walker · Rhiannon Armstrong · Rhodri Jones · Richard Dew · Richard Ellis · Richard Gwyn · Richard Major · Richard Martin · Richard Ross · Richard Smith · Richard Soundy · Richard Steward · Richard Hoey & Helen Crump · Rob Jefferson-Brown · Rob Plews · Robert Gillett · Robin Patterson · Robin Taylor · Robyn Neil · Ronan Cormacain · Ros Schwartz ·

Rose Cole · Rosemary Rodwell · Ross Macpherson · Roz Simpson · Rufus Johnstone · Rune Salvesen · Ruth Van Driessche · Ruth F Hunt · SE Guine · Sabine Griffiths · Sally Baker · Sam Cunningham · Sam Gordon · Sam Ruddock · Samantha Sabbarton-Wright · Samantha Schnee · Samantha Smith · Sandra de Monte · Sandra Hall · Sarah Benson · Sarah Butler · Sarah Kilvington · Sarah Lippek · Sarah Pybus · Sarah Salmon · Scott Beidler · Sean Malone · Sean McGivern · Seini O'Connor · Sez Kiss · Shaun Whiteside · Sheridan Marshall · Shirley Harwood · Sian O'Neill · Simon Armstrong · Simon Fay · Simon John Harvey · Simone O'Donovan · Siobhan Jones · Sioned Puw Rowlands · SJ Nevin · Sonia McLintock · Sophia Wickham · Steph Morris · Stephen Bass · Stephen Karakassidis · Stephen Pearsall · Stephen Walker · Stephen H Oakey · Steven Reid · Steven Williams · Steven & Gitte Evans · Sue Childs · Sue Eaglen and Colin Crewdson · Susan Lea · Susan Tomaselli · Susanna Jones · Susie Roberson · Suzanne Ross · Swithun Cooper · Sylvie Zannier-Betts · Tammi Owens · Tammy Harman · Tammy Watchorn · Tania Hershman · Tara Cheesman · Tehmina Khan · Thami Fahmy · The Mighty Douche Softball Team · The Rookery in the Bookery · Thea Bradbury · Thees Spreckelsen · Thomas Bell · Thomas Fritz · Thomas Mitchell · Tien Do · Tim Jackson · Tim Theroux · Tim Warren · Timothy Harris · Tina Rotherham-Winqvist · Tom Bowden · Tom Darby · Tom Franklin · Tom Mandall · Tony Bastow · Tony & Joy Molyneaux · Tracy Bauld · Tracy Lee-Newman · Tracy Northup · Trevor Lewis · Trevor Wald · Trevor Wald · Troy Zabel · Val Challen · Vanessa Nolan · Veronica Cockburn · Vicky Grut · Victoria Adams · Victoria Walker · Visaly Muthusamy · Vivien Doornekamp-Glass · Wendy Langridge · Wendy Patterson · Wenna Price · Will Huxter · William Powell · William G Dennehy · Yukiko Hiranuma · Zac Palmer · Zoë Brasier ·

One year she used a stainless steel one, but never again. She hated the idea she could accidentally catch the light or a glimpse of something in the side of it. It also gave her memories of very bad tea brewed in such teapots at weddings and funerals. Since life was a daily funeral, she didn't turn out for many of them. She only went to funerals where she suspected the person had a good reason to have a grudge against her on account of Martin John. She knew that her absence would suggest guilt.

She always took communion at those funerals and she attended every stage of the mourning. She could imagine a slim crowd at her own funeral. She could see Martin John going to the grave with no one at his funeral. They might go together and make it easy on all.

But her thoughts are now disordered. She has a final note to place inside this grubby-looking teapot and she has to seal it closed. She won't open another teapot this way she decides. That's it for the *pot, pot, pots* as she calls them.

After she put Martin John in the Chair she knew there was no further use for the teapots. What would you be doing firing things into them after that? Ask yourself.

---→

WHAT THEY KNOW:

The railway stations.

There aren't so many details on what Martin John exactly and precisely did at an obscure railway station in Hertfordshire, England, but it is supposed by mam he was visiting Noanie or on his way home from visiting her when *it* happened.

Whatever he did—and mam suspects some kind of exposure or tip slip because of his proximity to the litter bin —led to his removal to hospital where the phone calls recommenced.

What did you do? mam asks him before squealing twice as loud, *I don't want to know. Save me from it, d'ya hear? Get yourself out of there. Get yourself out of there. Get out and visit Noanie on Wednesday.*